JOSEPH OF NAZARETH

a novel

MICHAEL D. BRITTON

For Jean & Seth

CONTENTS

Acknowledgements

I'm grateful for the support of my lovely wife Jean, our precious son Seth, and my good friends Ryan Pitt & Matt Ballard. These faithful family and friends have provided so much more than first reading duties; they have provided love, moral support, and encouragement. I'm also grateful to my Father in Heaven for prompting me to switch gears in my writing career and create a piece of religious historical fiction – not something that had previously been on my agenda.

Cover design by Sue Gagnier
Cover model: Aaron Lambert
Cover model photography by Brett Stagg

PROLOGUE

"My son," I whispered.

Cold, hard raindrops from the darkening, roiling heavens pelted the ground all around me, somehow missing my tan, wrinkled face. But my cheeks were bathed in salty tears that streamed uncontrollably from my stinging eyes.

My eyes, mercifully, were too wet to see clear details of the awful scene which lay before me, a short distance away at the place they called *Golgotha*.

Despite the aching in my soul, I couldn't pull myself away – as if it were my duty to force myself to watch this horrific event to the bitter end. I stared toward the hill as the sky grew an even deeper shade of gray – my stomach tight, my labored breathing ragged and shallow.

The wind picked up, and I instinctively wrapped my robe more tightly around my wiry body, though I could barely feel the sudden cold that swept from the heavens, accompanied by a fierce howling.

In the crowd, I could see a number of people I knew. Some were jeering and taunting, and even, to my utter disgust, laughing. Others – family members, the Marys, some staunch disciples, those who had been called to the ministry, and those with just a glimmer of belief beginning to blossom – were overcome with crippling grief as they stood by, powerless to change this torturous destiny.

And if it was this bad for me – knowing what I know – it had to be absolutely devastating for them.

The indigo sky rumbled and bellowed, a parable of the cries from the darkened hearts of those mourning. My soul was in knots of turmoil as I felt more helpless than at any time during my life. I knew this had to be – and I understood that this was not the end – but that didn't make it any easier to watch.

My sickened, agonized heart longed to join the group of followers, to put my arm around my noble wife, Mary – to commiserate.

But I knew I could not.

Besides, John – blessed John – was there comforting my Mary now.

Most of the mocking from the riotous, bloodthirsty mob had ceased at this point – they'd grown tired of their sport and began murmuring among themselves, many wandering off, becoming bored and wishing to escape the thickening rain and biting gusts of wind. Only the faithful, and a few Roman soldiers – remaining to fulfill their ghastly duty – braved the weather now.

Lightning continued to flash in the low hills around Jerusalem, briefly illuminating the olive groves and painting a milky white glow across the faces of those gathered for the crucifixion – short bursts of brightness cutting through the ever-darkening heavens.

As I squinted at the bleeding man nailed mercilessly to the center of the three crosses, his life ebbing away under strained breaths, my mind was carried away in memories – memories of a life so great, so perfect – and so short.

As I peered through the rain, I saw Jesus' lips move. He seemed to say, "It is finished." Then his head sagged forward, and he was still.

A solemn wail emanated from the group of followers, and the clouds above boomed thunderously as nature herself groaned in savage agony.

A rush of heavy raindrops furiously showered the whole land.

My chest abruptly hollow, I gulped hard and again whispered, "My son."

CHAPTER I – FALLING FOR MARY

A gentle breeze carried the faint scent of dates and rustled the leaves of a nearby olive tree, causing the shadows to dance playfully on the dusty ground below. The air was warm, and quite humid for this early in the season. I could hear the murmurs of the other apprentices in nearby workspaces – stone rooms set into a larger stone structure where several men shared water and other resources for their humble businesses.

Not far from the market at the center of the village, this location served as a sort of school for me as I prepared to one day take my place as a carpenter. The other apprentices in the open-fronted building quietly learned from their own craftsman fathers: some fashioning brass, others creating hinge-pins, some working with stone.

"Joseph, please pay attention," my father said, reaching out and shaking my shoulder. "This is important."

I knew it was important. He was passing along to me intricate details and knowledge of his trade. This mattered, especially to me now, at age seventeen. Although I'd already been working with my father for years, very soon I would need to support myself at this trade – and a wife and family. Understanding the family business was a necessity, and before long I'd be far more than a mere apprentice.

My eyes followed the young woman walking past, lingering on her shiny black hair for only a moment before I turned back to my father. I shielded my eyes from the late afternoon sun that beamed down from above the thatched roof. "I'm sorry, Father, I was just –"

"You were just distracted by one of many possible futures, Joseph," Father said sternly, though not unkindly. He almost seemed to be suppressing a smile as he chastised me. "But the present requires your careful attention if you could hope to have any such future, you understand?"

"Yes, Father," I said, meeting his dark brown eyes before looking back down at the large timber he was manipulating with a shaving blade. "That young woman," I said tentatively, "do you know her parents?"

"Of course. I know nearly everyone in Nazareth. I also know that she is already betrothed to Isaac's son, Asher."

"Asher?" I said, shocked. "But he's betrothed to Ruth, the daughter of Ibrahim."

"Not anymore," said Father. He lowered his voice. "She was found to be unworthy. Asher put her away."

I looked down and gulped. "Did they . . . stone her?"

Father scratched at his white beard, staring out into the distance. "This is what I have been told. I do not participate in the stonings. I know they are *formally* lawful, according to the way our neighbors misinterpret God's word, but they profoundly disturb me and fill me with disgust. It deeply saddens me to see how far our people have fallen from the God who gave them life." He paused for a moment, then said, "Remember, Joseph – our neighbors are good people, but they often do bad things, falsely in the name of God. But this is between you and me. I do not wish to stir up trouble."

With that, he returned to delicately shaving fine strips from the wooden beam, releasing the aroma of fresh-cut wood that I had come to love, and I paid close attention as he demonstrated the proper technique.

Father did know most people in Nazareth. He was not a friend to everyone – not in the sense that he had intimate dealings with many – though he was friendly to all. His experience with the people of our small town arose primarily from having lived here most of his life, and from being the best local carpenter. At one time or another, nearly everyone had had need of his services working with wood. He was also very faithful in his periodic service at the synagogue, and knew personally a few of the priests.

Father handed me the shaving tool, and I began to pull it across the beam toward my body using both hands. As he had shown me, I kept it level and made smooth, steady motions with each stroke. Small slivers of the pale yellow wood leapt from the blade and gently fell upon my tanned, muscled forearms with each pass.

This kind of work allowed for much thinking. I thought about Ruth, and my heart ached. I really did not know her that well – I only knew she was tall, fair-skinned, and liked to laugh. The idea of that young woman having been struck dead by a hail of rocks – it was hard to bear – hard to believe such a barbaric practice could be legal. I did know Asher – and I knew him to be an honorable man. He was a year older than me, the son of a cask-maker, and quite eager to fulfill his responsibility to marry. I know he had cared for Ruth. I wondered how he felt about her stoning. As his family had already initiated a new betrothal for him, his acceptance of the situation was probably, sadly, complete. Either that, or he was just trying not to think about it and move on.

I know God has His reasons for allowing tragedies and atrocities to come to pass at the hands of wicked or misguided people. The idea that they do these things claiming that God condones – or even commands them – is an insult to my God. I know He has a plan, but sometimes I wish I could better understand why he refrains from intervening. I do not understand how, in this corrupt world, justice and mercy can both be attributes of divinity, operating at the same time. The concept confuses me such that I would rather not think about it – but I cannot help but ponder on it sometimes.

"Joseph – please focus on the work," said Father.

"You are digging too deeply into the edges of the beam. I can tell you are very distracted today. Let us take a break."

I handed him the blade, and he hung it on the wall, then sat down heavily on one of two low, broad stumps in the corner. "Bring some water," he said, gesturing with his hand.

"Yes, Father."

I grabbed two small earthen cups kept on the shelf and stepped into the common area to the water trough. It was filled from the well each morning, and used by all of us in the craftsman shops throughout the day. By this time of the afternoon, having been in the sun all day, it was not cool at all – but it was wet, and that's what mattered.

I handed Father a cup and sat down beside him with my own, sipping at the tepid liquid.

"What troubles you, Joseph?" he asked, after taking a long swig of the water. "Are you upset by the news of Ruth?"

I nodded. "Yes. But that is not all."

"You are concerned about your own status. You wish to marry. I know this, Joseph."

He was right – I was worried about my near future. Rather than discuss with him what was really bothering me – my questions about justice and mercy – I decided to talk about the other subject. "I should marry soon, yet I have no prospects. Most of the eligible young women in Nazareth are already betrothed."

Or dead.

Father gazed outside, squinting at the bright sunlight reflected off the other stone structures nearby. "This evening, you will meet your future wife."

My heart leapt. Was this prophecy?

"How? How do you know?"

"We will have visitors tonight for supper – my cousin Amram and his family. He has a fair daughter, Mary."

"Mary?" I asked, surprised. "She is already of marrying age?"

"She turned fourteen a season ago. Time takes wing, my son."

Indeed it does. I was aware of young Mary – always a sweet little girl – but did not realize she was already fourteen. "So," I ventured, "have there already been . . . arrangements made? Between you and your cousin?"

"Amram and I will hopefully begin working that out tonight. Now, shall we finish this beam?"

He clapped his hands on his knees and stood, and I immediately followed, placing my cup down on the stump and enthusiastically taking hold of the blade, ready to focus on my work.

The sky outside was not yet totally dark – a rich spectrum of red, purple and indigo illuminated the western horizon as the stars began to appear in the deeper darkness overhead and to the east.

A mouthwatering aroma filled our home as Mother placed two lit earthenware lamps on our low dining table, spaced about an arm's length apart. Thin wisps of oil-smoke rose from the tip of each vessel's flame as it danced atop the flax wick. The light cast multiple shadows and caused the hewn stone walls of our dining area to glow a warm orange-crimson.

Father stood facing the table, counting his fingers with his eyes cast upward. "Sariah," he finally said to one of my sisters, "please bring one more lambskin and one more cup and plate to the table."

"I'll fetch the lambskin," I said, walking out of the dining room to retrieve another place to sit from my parents' room.

Soon, Amram's family would arrive – including Mary, the woman my father said I would marry. Tonight, perhaps, I would learn what much of the rest of my life would be like. As long as Father and his cousin could come to a satisfactory agreement.

As I hurried back from the other room with a lambskin in my arms, I heard the guests arriving. I patted my hair down, then straightened my robe. I ran my hand across my chin, feeling the soft beginnings of my beard, hoping it did not make me appear too much like a boy.

"Amram," my father said with a welcoming tone, "it has been too long."

I entered the front room with the lambskin and saw a tall, slender man with long white beard crossing the threshold. I quickly placed the lambskin at the dining table and returned to the entry area.

"It is good to see you again, Heli," said Amram to my father.

"Joseph, go out and help with the animals," said Father.

I bowed respectfully to Amram as I passed him and went outside to assist with Amram's family pack animals. I led two asses around to the back of our home and into a small corral, making sure there was adequate water and hay for them to eat.

I returned to the front in time to help a young woman down from her mount.

"Here," I said, extending my hand to the woman, whose head was covered by a soft brown veil.

"Thank you," she said, taking my hand and stepping down.

As her weight shifted toward me, my foot slipped in a patch of wet dung.

I struggled to stay upright, my only thought to protect the girl from falling onto the dirty ground.

Faster than I could think, it was over: I lay flat on my back in the dust. To my great relief, the young woman stood above me, perfectly composed and unharmed.

"Thank you," she said again, this time extending her hand to me, that I might be lifted up.

I took it, but used my own strength to stand. I was then face to face with her – still grasping her delicate hand.

Her gentle smile was radiant, and seemed to blow away my embarrassment like a gust of summer breeze.

Her beauty made me catch my breath. Then I realized.

"Mary."

"Yes, it's me," she said, still smiling. "Were you expecting someone else?"

"Um, no – of course not. I just – I hadn't realized you – I – you've grown since I last saw you."

She blushed a little, and said, "So have you."

With that, I grabbed the large pouch from the back of her animal and we turned toward the house. "Oh!" I said, stopping. "I need to put your donkey in the back with the others. You may go on into the house – I'll be right back."

Still clutching her pouch, I led the animal to the back, looking back to see Mary enter the house before I rounded the corner.

I had not expected young Mary to be such a fine young woman. I had not really anticipated anything – but this came as a true surprise. And she had a penetrating serenity about her – a calm strength that emanated from her face, from her eyes. She exuded purity and goodness, like no other woman I had ever met.

As I returned to the house and entered the door, everyone seemed to be staring at me. I looked down at the pouch in my hand. "I'm sorry," I said, extending my arm to Mary, "this is yours."

"Actually," said Amram, "it is *yours*. Mary was to present it to you as a token of gratitude for your hospitality tonight and your interest in a future together."

I looked down. "Oh. I apologize."

"None needed, young Joseph," said Amram, the hint of a smile tickling the corners of his thin lips. "You were just helping."

We all stood there – the two families – for a few moments of silence. Finally, my father broke the spell and said, "Well, son, *open* it!"

I reached into the sack and my fingers found a hard object, which I extracted. I turned it over in my hands, and quickly recognized it.

"A mortise gauge! This is very nice," I said.

"Excellent!" said Father. "Every carpenter needs his own personal mortise gauge. Very thoughtful."

"Yes, thank you, very much," I said.

"And we have something for Mary," said Mother, stepping behind my father to a shelf cut into the stone wall. "A gift from our family," she said, handing the object to Mary.

Mary looked at the fine-twined linen headscarf with reverent awe.

"This is beautiful," she said. "Thank you. I will wear it the next time I am sewing the veils in the temple."

"Come, let us wash and eat," said Father merrily.

We adjourned to the dining room, and sat down on the soft lambskins on the floor surrounding the table.

My sisters exited to the kitchen and returned quickly carrying bowls of water which they placed at the feet of each guest before gently and respectfully washing the feet of the visitors.

Once the washing was complete, they took the bowls away and returned with plates of flatbread, boiled veal, figs and grape juice.

As head of the guest family, Amram was served first – the honored guest receiving the largest portion of meat; then my father was served, then the rest of Amram's family, and lastly ours.

We washed our hands in the small, shallow bowls on the table before each of us, and Father pronounced a traditional blessing before we took up the food and ate.

"Heli," said Amram, leaning on one elbow and taking a sip of juice, "your son has grown into a fine young man."

Mary glanced over to me briefly, a light smile playing at the corners of her mouth. I felt my heart begin to pound in my chest. Only a few hours ago, I was lamenting my lack of marital prospects, and now I found myself seated at a meal with this amazing young woman, while her father spoke well of me. Could this really be happening?

"Indeed he has, Cousin," said my father, plucking a grape from its stem and popping it in his mouth. "He is a good worker, and faithfully attends synagogue. I have taught him well – ha!"

Father chuckled jovially, and Amram joined in.

Mother looked directly at Father, not saying a word, but her eyes seemed to make him fidget. After a moment, he stopped chuckling and said with a serious voice, but a twinkle in his eye, "Of course, I taught him many things – but Joseph is certainly the good man he is because of the profound influence of his good mother."

Seemingly satisfied, Mother returned to her food with a small nod of acknowledgement.

The subtle, good-natured wrangling between my parents distracted me momentarily from the fact that I was being praised. I was quickly reminded when Amram spoke next.

"Yes," he said seriously, placing his cup on the table, "Joseph would make a fine husband, and I'm sure an excellent father, too. As you know, my daughter Mary has reached the appropriate age for marriage."

"Indeed," said Father, "that is something I had hoped to discuss with you this evening. I know it is customary to conduct these negotiations at your home, but since you are here, perhaps now would be a convenient opportunity to come to an arrangement."

Amram gently twisted the long white hairs of his beard, pondering.

I held my breath.

Finally, he responded. "It is well. I understand this is your busy season for construction – you need not make the journey to my home to discuss this matter, when we are already here tonight."

Mary and her family did not live very far away – only a few miles outside of town. But Amram was right – Father had much work to do these next few weeks, as the weather was now ideal outdoor woodworking conditions. He had little spare time for family visits such as would normally be expected for the arrangement of a betrothal. I took heart; perhaps by the end of this night, I would be one very important step closer to having a wife.

To having Mary.

I looked over at her, and she seemed to glow with a perfect radiance and a placid joy – so beautiful, so virtuous.

"We have saved up a considerable sum," said Father. "We believe it should be an ample and honorable compensation."

"You should know," said Amram, "that Mary is a very hard worker. Not only does she serve many hours helping sew veils in the temple during the off-season, but at home she cooks, she cleans, she helps with the animals. She is worth two strong men, or a dozen docile girls. She will make a faithful wife and a great contribution to your family. And she will be sorely missed."

And so the negotiation began.

"Of course," said Father. "I assumed Mary to be an impeccable young woman. This is why the amount we offer is so substantial."

I looked back at Mary once more, and she was engaged in a quiet side conversation with one of my sisters, Deborah. For a few moments, while my father and his cousin haggled over the price of this arrangement, I was lost in thought, wondering what our life together would be like. We'd live near here – I already had a plot of land selected at the far end of Father's property upon which I would build our home. There would be children soon – but how soon, and how many? Boys, girls? How would I grow and change as I got to know Mary better? And would she change – or would she ever retain that beautiful purity and faithfulness? Would she get along well with my mother? Would I be successful as a carpenter, able to provide well for our family? So many questions – so many years to find the answers. Together.

I heard my sister whisper, "He's staring at you again."

Mary looked over at me and smiled. Then she said, just loud enough for me to hear, "Yes, he is, isn't he?"

I felt my face flush, and reached for my cup, taking a long swig of grape juice. As I placed the cup back on the table, my father announced, "Then it is done! There will be a betrothal!"

I gulped the last of the juice that was in my mouth, caught my breath, and looked back across the table at the woman who was to be my wife.

Mary.

\#

The weeks between the arrangement and the betrothal ceremony seemed to pass as an instant before my eyes; while at the same time, it felt like a generation.

I would wake up and go to work with my father. We would speak of various things while he trained me, as we always did. But at the end of the day, I could never recall what we had spoken of, nor really remember what techniques I had learned or practiced that day.

Though I surely must have seemed inattentive or distracted, Father did not chastise me.

One particularly hot afternoon, just a few days before the ceremony was to take place, Father suggested we take a water break and sat down to speak with me, much the same way as he had on the day the betrothal had been arranged.

"Joseph," he said, mopping his brow with the back of his dirty hand and exhaling. He looked me squarely in the eye. "I know you have been somewhat preoccupied as the day of your betrothal approaches."

"I'm sorry, Father. I – "

"No, no," Father said, waving his hand. "It is all right. I understand. I was nervous before I married your mother. You have much on your mind these days. Have you any . . . questions?"

I gulped at the water, thirsty from the work of the day. "Only one, Father. When will you help me begin building my house?"

He smiled at me. I think he was relieved,

somehow. "After the betrothal ceremony," he said. "The day after."

"Will there be sufficient time to complete it, you know – before the wedding?"

"Of course! We will have plenty of time. Your wedding will not be for several months. It shall all come together – you'll see. By the time you are married, you will have a roof over your head and some land for a few animals – everything you need. Do not worry."

Father was good at that – helping to make people feel comfortable. And it worked for me. I took a deep breath and said, "Thank you. I am ready to complete our tasks for today."

"Good," said Father. "Because after you finish shaving that tenon and fitting it into the mortise, you'll be done. With everything."

"Everything?"

"Yes. That is the last of your education, Joseph. If you put that joint together tightly with no flaws, you will know all that I know – you will be a master carpenter."

"But – but I'm not ready –"

"Yes, yes you are, my son. You are ready to do your own work for your own customers. You have accomplished much – these past few weeks especially." He grinned at me. "Must be the motivation."

I turned my mortise gauge over in my hands, examining the fine details of the tool. The tool Mary's family had given me. "I suppose so," I said. "Father? Do you think I am also ready for this next step in my life – to become a husband, eventually a father – to become my own man?"

He placed his rough hand firmly on my shoulder and looked in my eyes. "Joseph, I have no idea what kind of a life awaits you with Mary. She is a wonderful virgin, and I'm sure your life together will be rewarding. And whatever comes your way, I am confident that you are prepared. Now – how about you finish fitting that joint together?"

Mary looked even more perfect than at our last meeting, the night our betrothal had been arranged. And tonight, the negotiations of that evening would come to fruition.

Mary's long, shiny dark hair flowed straight down from under her veil. Her skin seemed to glow by the light of the late evening sun and the flame sconces in the courtyard of her father's home. Her hands looked so soft, despite the diligent work she used them for on a daily basis. She stood straight as a beam alongside her father, awaiting the officiating of the ceremony.

Amram's home was a brown stone structure, squat for the most part, except for a raised area toward the back. It was of medium size and well-kept. The courtyard on the side of the house, where we held the betrothal ceremony, was comprised of three low hewn-rock walls with a cistern in one corner. Along the house wall, pegs stuck out where various tools hung. Along the other two walls, several olive trees hung over from the outside, providing a small amount of shade. The air was warm and still, and smelled of the meat cooking within the home.

I looked up at the eastern sky, where the heavens grew a deep purple, and saw the first star of the night appear before my eyes. I took it as a good sign.

There were not many people present – just Amram's family, which consisted of Amram and his wife, and Mary and her five siblings; my father's family, which included Mother, Father, me, and my brothers and sisters; plus a friend of Mary's named Chloe, and a friend of my father named Malachi, with his son Dovev.

Dovev was about ten years my senior – and was soon to be inducted into the Sanhedrin as a Pharisee. And he was quickly becoming my best friend.

Finally, the last guest was Rabbi Hebor.

"Let us begin," said Amram. He introduced Rabbi Hebor, who began speaking to the assembled group.

I can hardly remember the details of the ceremony itself – it seemed to all happen so quickly, yet as I looked at Mary, I felt suspended in time. I tried hard to listen to the words Rabbi Hebor said, but I just couldn't seem to focus. Much like the time spent with my father near the end of my apprenticeship, I must have been absorbing what was going on around me while my mind and spirit clung to thoughts of Mary.

I do recall Rabbi Hebor saying something about the importance of marriage in God's eternal plan. He spoke some words from the scriptures. He then blessed us, and we committed our vows with a simple "Yes," to each of his questions for us.

The good rabbi verified that both fathers approved of the match, and then pronounced a final brief blessing, "May you both find a marriage of joy like no other."

And it was done.

Rabbi Hebor placed Mary's hand in mine, and squeezed them together with his wrinkled palm.

We turned to face our families and guests, smiling.

From this day forward, we were legally bound.

United.

Come what may.

The remainder of the evening was occupied by the feast. So much delicious food: roasted veal, quail and partridge; spiced lentil porridge, figs, pomegranates, honeycomb, grapes, fresh-baked bread, curd. And an unusual treat: watermelons.

And then there was the music and dancing. Of course, the men danced separate from the women, but that didn't stop Mary and I from watching each other from across the courtyard throughout the festivities.

The festivities reached well toward midnight before everyone tired and decided it was time to leave. Before Dovev left, he came and took me by the shoulders, then embraced me.

He was a tall man of strong build, with curly black hair and a sparkle in his eyes.

"Well done, my friend," he said. "You have been betrothed to the finest virgin in Nazareth. You will do well together. She is clearly a virtuous and faithful woman."

"Thank you, Dovev," I said. "I am well pleased, indeed."

"And when will she be leaving her father's house to join you in the home you shall build?"

"The wedding? That is not for another five months."

"You'd better get building, friend!" Dovev laughed. "That time will go quickly."

"Actually, my father and I are starting tomorrow."

"Let me know if you need any help. I'll be sure to find you someone who enjoys working in the heat." Dovev smiled and slapped me on the shoulder, then departed with his father.

I grinned as he left, then turned and saw Mary as she helped her friend Chloe get settled for the night just inside the house. Mary then emerged and walked toward me.

"Joseph," she said, taking my hand and looking into my eyes, "I am so very happy tonight."

"As am I, Mary."

She gazed up at the heavens, now liberally dotted with stars – some tiny pinpricks of light, others shimmering and bright against the black velvet universe.

"You are a good man, and I will be a good wife to you."

"I know you will, Mary," I said. "I am a very blessed man."

"Tomorrow you and your father begin building, yes?"

I nodded. "Yes. I have it all planned out. There will be much to do, but it will be very nice when it's all done."

"Then you had better get to sleep," she said, squeezing my hand. "Your family is all situated in the back room. I hope you will be comfortable."

"Thank you." I looked around us. Everybody else had retired for the night. I took the opportunity of privacy to give Mary a quick embrace. "Good night."

"Good night, my espoused."

CHAPTER II – SILENT SCANDAL &
VOCAL REVELATION

Every day for the next six weeks, Mary came and visited the worksite where my father and I labored to craft the timbers for what would be our home.

She brought water and food and kindly tended to our every comfort and physical need, ensuring we did not get too hot or too thirsty or too fatigued. Her willingness to serve and her good humor made the work so much lighter, and made the days pass with haste. Her smile brightened each morning and brought each evening to a pleasant close.

In the next few days, I would bring in more help as we began more of the heavy lifting, but for now, it was just Father and I, and my lovely espoused wife in support.

The land here was nearly flat, and I had already cleared away the scrub brush from the level spot where the house would sit. In the distance, I could see the animal stalls of my father's home. Behind us to the west lay the low hills of Runa'an Salah, dotted with low trees. It was a nice location, one I knew we would be happy in as we raised our family.

And the work was progressing quite well.

Then one day, Mary did not come.

This worried me, as her daily visits had become very routine, but I tried to just focus on the work, and not let my mind make up unpleasant reasons for her absence.

"I hope she is not ill," said Father, around noon.

"As do I," I said. "Perhaps we can finish early today, and I will visit her home to make sure she is all right."

"You are the boss on this job," said Father. "You do as you please."

This was a bit of a turnaround for me. I'd spent my whole life working for my father, and was always subject to his decisions.

"Very well, then," I said, taking a breath, along with the initiative, "let's finish for today. I am concerned, and would like to visit Mary and be able to return before the sun sets."

Father nodded, put down his tools, and mopped his brow. "Go on then – I'll clean up."

"Thank you," I said, and hurried off.

I kept my pace quick, only pausing briefly to quench my thirst at the community well as I passed through the center of Nazareth. The bright yellow sun, directly overhead, beat down on my head and shoulders relentlessly as I continued on out of the village toward Mary's family's home.

When I finally arrived at the edge of the

property, I saw Mary sitting under a tree, looking well enough, but with a curious expression of faraway pondering on her face. She was so lost in thought that she did not even notice my arrival until I was close enough to startle her.

"Mary."

"Oh, Joseph!" she said, shaking herself. "I'm sorry – I – I didn't see you."

I knelt down beside her, still catching my breath from the brisk hike. "Are you all right? My father and I were expecting you today, as you have come each day. Do you feel well? You seem . . . troubled."

Mary looked down and said nothing for a few moments. Then a tear came to her eye, glistening in the sun as she looked over at me. "I am not unwell."

"Are you certain? Why did you not come today?"

A tear slid down Mary's cheek. "I – I cannot say." She placed her hands across her belly and laced her fingers, and slowly shook her head.

"I've not seen you like this before," I said, getting even more concerned. "If you are not sick, or mourning, why can you not tell me what is wrong? Have you decided you do not wish to marry me?"

"Oh, no, Joseph! It is not that. I do wish to marry you." She looked away, to the horizon. "I hope you still wish to marry me."

Now I was truly confused. "Of course I do. Nothing has changed."

Mary stood. "I must go." She walked toward her home, leaving me there on the ground, wondering what could possibly be happening. I watched her enter the home and shut the door gently.

I sat there, the breeze picking up and blowing my hair, staring at her father's house. I wondered if women were always so mysterious. I stood and walked away, back to my father's house, my head down and my mind swimming.

I did not speak much the rest of the day.

The next day, I had difficulty rising and getting to work. I felt like I weighed as much as an ox, and I could not concentrate on anything.

"Joseph," Father said early in the day as we lifted a timber onto a sawhorse, "what is the matter? You never told me what is wrong with Mary. Is she well?"

I did not meet my father's gaze. "No. I mean, yes. She says she is well. I do not know."

"Either she is well or she is not. How is it that you do not know? You spoke with her, yes?"

"I did. But I came away knowing less than I did before we spoke."

My father, to my surprise, broke into a grin. "Ah, I see. So, you are beginning to learn the ways of a woman!"

I shook my head. "No, I – I just do not understand."

Father came and placed a hand on my shoulder. "Do not worry, Joseph. In fact, I would be worried if you *did* understand every mood and thought of a woman." He smiled again. "Put it out of your mind. In a few days all will be clear, smooth, and wonderful again."

I struggled to not think any more on the subject, but could not seem to erase from my mind the image of Mary's peculiar countenance, the way she seemed both burdened and unconcerned all at once.

I slept little that night. By the time the first hints of false dawn kissed the horizon, I had resolved to return to Mary and see if there was some way I could convince her to speak openly with me about what was going on.

At sunrise, I told my father I would not be at the worksite immediately, but later in the day. He was pleased, as he had business in Nazareth to tend to anyway.

As soon as I had eaten a little bread and grapes, I made my way hastily to Mary's father's house, my feet carrying me like a bird on the breeze, but my heart and mind heavy with questions and confusion.

When I approached the house, I saw that Mary was at the side fetching water from one of the great cisterns.

"Mary," I said, walking up to her. "Um, how are you feeling today?"

She turned, and her face was radiant for an instant, but quickly shadowed by a look I could not define. Pity? Remorse? It was unclear exactly what it was – but it made my heart sink.

"Hello, Joseph," she said, tentatively. She opened her mouth as if to speak again, then closed it. After a deep breath, she said, "Joseph, we need to talk."

So, I would not have to pry it out of her – she was going to tell me what this was all about. "Yes,"

I said. "Where shall we go?"

"Let's walk out to the tree where you saw me the other day."

We walked in silence, and Mary sat down upon the ground, her back to the tree, much as she had been when I came to her before.

"So," I said, sitting before her on the ground. The morning sun upon my back was warm, and bathed Mary in a yellow glow that seemed to make her perfect skin shine. "Tell me, Mary, what is the matter? Why did you stop coming to the house, and why would you not speak with me the other day when I came to see if you were well?"

Mary's eyes once more became wet, and she seemed to struggle for words. Finally, she spoke.

"Oh, Joseph. Joseph, I am . . . with child."

She placed her hand gently on her belly. She seemed so calm – almost happy.

I stood up, shocked. My legs felt weak, but I remained on my feet and started pacing.

"You're – you're what? With child? But – but how? I mean, Mary!"

My heart leapt and sank, my stomach felt sick. I felt dizzy. This was impossible. My Mary? My espoused wife? My *virtuous* espoused wife – with *child*?

Tears filled my eyes. My breath grew short. Mary started to speak – to try to explain, but my ears seemed to close. All I could hear was my own heartbeat pounding in my head.

I turned and fled before she could say another word.

The run home was a blur.

I covered the distance at the top of my speed without stopping, and when I got back to my father's house, I went around to the back where we kept the animals, and collapsed in the hay.

I didn't want anyone to see me or talk to me.

My numb mind raced as my aching heart throbbed in my chest.

Just days ago, I was the happiest and most blessed man – and now, now I –

It was simply unbelievable.

A wave of emotions passed over me – anger, fear, disbelief, sadness. More disbelief.

It simply did not make sense.

If it were true – if Mary was with child – it broke my heart to think what would happen.

She would be stoned.

What was I to do?

I buried my head in my hands and wept.

After a few minutes, I caught my breath, and dropped to my knees. I poured my heart out to God. I asked if it were really true. I asked what I should do. I begged Him that somehow this could all be a dream.

I gained some strength from my prayer. I calmed down, and began to ponder the situation with more clarity.

I did not want this to be so, but what she had said was unmistakable. Mary was with child. We were not yet married. We had never even known each other! Which meant she had either betrayed me – which seemed impossible to imagine and too heavy to bear – or some foul brute had taken from her that which is precious. And that thought infuriated me.

But under either circumstance, by law, she would pay dearly.

Perhaps – perhaps I could put her away privately. No one would have to know. We could simply dissolve the betrothal and pretend it never happened – our families would have to keep it a secret forever. Keeping such a secret would be a great burden, if it were even possible. But it would save her life. And although I was pained by what had happened, and the woeful loss of my love and my planned future, I would rather Mary have another chance at life, than to suffer the cruel death of stoning at the hands of my fellow Nazarenes.

As I considered this possibility, I continued to keep a prayer in my heart. Perhaps, somehow, God could guide me in what to do.

My limbs were exhausted from my speedy retreat from Mary's father's home, and my mind was fatigued also. I felt a lump in my throat that would not go away. My eyes grew heavy, and as I lay on the hay in the shade, the gentle breeze on my face, I fell asleep.

When I awoke, it was evening.

I stood, my body aching, and staggered off to my father's house. He looked at me, but did not ask me any questions. He must have seen from my face that I was not ready to talk. The next several days passed in agonized silence as I rose, worked all day at building the house with no enthusiasm for the task – it felt futile – and barely said a word to my father, who alternated between looking concerned and trying to avoid my eyes. I wondered if he suspected anything.

Each night I prayed with all my strength for some sort of answers, some guidance in what to do. How could God have let this happen to Mary? She, who was so perfect, so lovely, so clean and decent and honorable? What kind of justice or mercy could be applied in such a circumstance?

One night, as my tears streamed down my face as I knelt prayer, I wondered how long I could go on feeling like this. I felt like I was at my breaking point. Many times, I had thought to speak with my father about it, but every time, something prevented me – it just didn't feel right. Now, with no one to turn to but my God, I begged and pleaded that he would provide me some comfort – some relief – from this torment.

Receiving none, I laid down to sleep, despairing I would never know what to do, and that it would become evident that Mary was with child, and that she would then be condemned.

But just as I was sinking into the darkness, a feeling of warmth and peace suddenly washed over me in the midst of that tension, and I was able to take a deep breath, let it out slowly, and drift off to sleep like a fast-moving river sliding by.

"Joseph. Joseph."

I looked up, and a magnificent man stood before me. His face shone above the brightness of the noonday sun, and his clothing was of the purest white, as nothing I had ever before seen. I felt a power move through my body and awaken all my senses. My mind was quickened, making me feel as if my everyday life were only a dream, while this was more real than anything.

At first, I feared – for I did not know who he was. I did not know what he was. But in an instant, as his eyes seemed to penetrate me, I felt no more fear. Only love.

Surely, I was dreaming.

"Who are you?" I asked.

"I am Gabriel. I have been sent by God to testify to you and to instruct you."

His voice was deep and rich, and seemed to touch my heart directly.

"Are you an answer to my prayer? About Mary?"

"Yes. Joseph, son of David, I say to you, do not fear to marry Mary: for that which is conceived in her is of the Holy Ghost. And she will bring forth a son, and you will call his name Jesus: for he will save his people from their sins."

I just stared at this heavenly messenger. I did not know what to say.

"Do you understand, Joseph? You are to take Mary to wife. She has not been untrue, and she has not been harmed. She bears the Messiah, the Lord Jesus Christ, of whom the prophets have spoken."

"I – I understand. And I believe."

"All this is done that it might be fulfilled which was spoken of the Lord by the prophet, who said, 'Behold, a virgin shall be with child, and shall bring forth a son, and they shall call his name Emmanuel, which being interpreted is, God with us.' Do you understand?"

"I know the scriptures, and I understand. A virgin shall be with child."

"Joseph, you are to take Mary to wife immediately, and know her not until she shall bring forth her firstborn son, the Holy One of Israel. Will you do this now?"

"Yes."

Gabriel, as this wondrous figure had called himself, then seemed to ascend into a bright light over my head.

I awoke with a start.

My mind felt sharp as a chisel, my breath steady.

Yet my body felt like I had fallen off the roof and been trampled by a camel. Sore and exhausted, as if I had run ten times the distance to Mary's. I willed myself to stand, despite my physically weak condition.

Oddly, the sun was already rising, as if my interview with the angel had occupied the entire night.

I stepped out of my father's house, and, placing one foot in front of the other, I started back toward Mary.

I felt bad for having left her like I had several days ago – not allowing her to explain, not saying good bye. I hoped she was not too worried.

Too worried! What was I thinking? She was carrying the Son of God in her womb! Of course she was worried.

And to top it off, her betrothed husband had fled from her sight like a child from a bear.

Poor, poor Mary!

I began to regain my strength, and quickened my pace.

As I ran, I wondered about all that had just transpired. I had seen and spoken with an angel of God! Why had God chosen us? Had a messenger also been sent to Mary, or was she scared and confused, wondering how she could be with child when she knew no man? No, surely God would have also spoken to her.

If only I had stayed and listened to her all those

days ago!

But – would I have even believed?

"Mary!" I called out as I approached her father's house, seeing her stepping into the home tending a flask of water. "Mary, wait."

She turned around.

Her face transformed from sadness to joy. She glowed as she broke into a smile.

"I can see from your face," she said as I stopped before her, "that you know."

I took her hands in mine. "Yes, yes I do know. An angel – "

"Was it Gabriel?"

"Yes!"

"He came to me, as well."

We strolled together back to the tree where we had spoken days ago, and sat on the ground in the shade of the morning sun. My heart seemed to be trembling with excitement now as she told me of her encounter with the messenger of God.

"It was several nights ago that he came to me. He was amazing – wasn't he?"

"Yes," I said, nodding, "so powerful and full of truth and beauty. Sent from the very God of heaven!"

"He said to me, 'Hail, Mary – you are highly favored, the Lord is with you and you are blessed among women.' I did not know what to say."

"I know – I was speechless at first, myself," I said.

"At first, I was troubled – I could not understand why this being should greet me that way. Then he said to me, 'Fear not, Mary, for you have found favor with God. And, behold, you will conceive in your womb, and bring forth a son, and will call his name Jesus. He will be great, and will be called the Son of the Highest, and the Lord God will give to him the throne of his father David, and he will reign over the house of Jacob forever; and of his kingdom there will be no end.' Of course, I was astonished, and said, 'How can this be, seeing I have not known a man?'"

I stared intently at Mary as she recounted the angelic visit, captivated by her bright eyes and the breathless nature of this life-changing story – a story so fantastic that I may have doubted it myself had I not just had a similar encounter.

Mary continued. "And the angel answered and said to me, 'The Holy Ghost will come upon you, and the power of the Highest will transfigure you: therefore the holy thing which will be born of you will be called the Son of God.'"

"That is what he told me, as well, Mary. The Son of God. Born of a virgin."

"Me," Mary said, tears welling up in her eyes.

"You."

"The angel also told me that my cousin, Elizabeth, has conceived a son in her old age – that she is now six months along! Joseph – Elizabeth was barren! But as the angel said to me, with God nothing is impossible."

"Nothing," I said, feeling a little bit of shock as the reality began to set in. "You, the virgin who will bear the Son of God. What did you say to Gabriel?"

"I did not know what else to say. I simply said, 'I am the handmaid of the Lord; let it be as you have said.' And then he departed from me. The vision was over. I felt exhilarated and exhausted all at once. I fell asleep, and when I awoke, I knew it had happened. I could feel the – the presence of the Lord. I knew that I carried a new life within me. But I did not know how to approach you, and I was still very tired, so I did not come to see you as I usually do. I am sorry I made you worry."

I put my hand on her shoulder. "It's all right, Mary. You have nothing to apologize for. I was a fool – I ran away from you, left you here. At first I was so confused, even angry. I am so sorry. I should have stayed and listened to you."

"I did not even know if I should tell you – I was not commanded either way. And if I had tried to explain to you – would you have believed me?"

I sighed. "I would like to think that I would have. You are an honest and pure woman. But I do not know – it is a lot to consider. I am glad God sent Gabriel to me as well, that we might have separate witnesses. And even if I had believed you – I would not have known what to do. But Gabriel instructed me – he told me that I must take you to wife – immediately."

"Joseph – what of our families? I was not told whether we can tell them about this sacred thing."

"Nor was I. I know we can trust them, but – I don't know. It does not feel right. For now, let us keep this to ourselves."

"How will you explain that you want to marry me immediately?"

"It has been several weeks since our betrothal – we are within the normal time for marriage. I know I had said I wanted to finish our house first, but – well, you have been coming out to our property every day, why should you have to keep making that journey, when you could just move into my father's house until our house is completed?"

"That is a very good reason. And it has the benefit of being true."

"Yes, it is true. Now, more than ever, I am concerned for you making the trek to our house each day. I needn't tell anyone why I am now particularly worried for you, only that I want you to be near, now. It is enough. As my father has told me, I am the boss now. I can make decisions for myself – for us. For our family."

Mary clasped my hand tightly and smiled gently. "We will be married."

"Straight away."

CHAPTER III – MARRIAGE AND A JOURNEY

I walked home quickly to tell my family. By the time I arrived, the sun was low in the sky, creating golden and red hues across the horizon. A cool breeze from the north brought the scent of my mother's cooking to my nose many paces before I reached the house.

I stepped inside and found my father, and announced without ceremony that I wished to get married to Mary the next day.

"Married?" asked Father. "Immediately? Why?"

It was very hard to not tell him of the angelic visit, of Mary's condition. But it did feel right, for now, to not speak of it. Hoping to somehow account for the last several days of anguish and confusion, I said, "She has grown weary of the daily journey to our house construction. The journey consumes a part of her day that leaves her wanting for time to complete her own chores at home. But she still wants to continue to serve us each day as we work on the house. I agree it is far for her to come every day, and that it would be advantageous to have her here, able to do the work of *your* home, instead of her father's early in the morning and late into the night. Why not just bring her into your home, that we may begin our life together now? It is not important that the new house be complete first."

Father looked at me sternly, as if searching for something in my mind by boring into my eyes. He surely knew that I was not telling him the entire story. He had seen the way I was acting the last few days – distraught and quiet. He knew his son. But, after what felt like several minutes of his silent scrutiny, he said tersely, "Very well. Send for the rabbi. Alert Mary's family. It shall be done as you wish."

I exhaled a long breath I had not realized I was holding. "Thank you, Father. Thank you."

He said nothing. I was grateful he did not question me further as to why it had to be immediately. I hoped he suspected nothing untoward. I would rather share our sacred visitation against my better judgment, than have Father think anything evil of Mary. But for now, it seemed the marriage would go forward in the morning – in keeping with the command of the angel – with no more questions asked.

After the evening meal, I set about putting everything in order. I walked into Nazareth and contacted Rabbi Hebor for a morning appointment. Then I paid a visit once more to Mary's father's home, where I told Mary that my father had assented, and that her family was invited to join ours at my father's home three hours after sunrise.

I also told her she should bring her personal belongings. Tomorrow, she would be my wife, and live with me in my father's home.

The usual excitement and special feelings associated with marriage were greatly overshadowed for both of us by the sacred trust we shared. A secret that seemed impossible to comprehend – a private miracle made real by our mutual experience of speaking with an angel of God.

The next morning, our guests arrived.

Mary's family all looked a little annoyed – particularly her father – understandable given the short notice. But as they got settled in and we all started talking, the edge of the mood seemed to be softened. Rabbi Hebor's arrival put us all in a good spirit, and the ceremony commenced in as normal a fashion as can be expected, given the unusual circumstance.

The day was beautiful – sunny, but not too hot. A warm breeze blew throughout the morning. Mother had somehow managed to find some flowers to decorate the outside of our home, and Father had arranged for additional refreshments to be carried in from the village – though no wine was available on such short notice.

Mary and I stood beside each other, still reeling from the sacred events of the previous day. Rabbi Hebor pronounced us husband and wife with fewer words than he had betrothed us. It was short, simple, and sweet. I still cannot really remember exactly what he said, so excited was my mind.

Suddenly, we were married.

The traditional wedding feast was considerably less elaborate than usual, given my mother had hardly had any time to prepare. We enjoyed some pheasant, a little lamb, some figs, dates and apples, and much grape juice.

I watched as my father and Amram spoke cordially, no doubt finalizing the business end of the arrangement. Mary's mother and mine also seemed to get along well, speaking together with all the daughters and laughing from time to time.

After only a few hours, Mary's family packed up and returned home, Father went into Nazareth to attend to his own work, and I helped Mary get settled in at my father's house – her new home, for now.

I set her few things down in a corner of the small back room that we would now share. "Well, here we are," I said.

"Here we are." She sat on the collection of bedclothes on the floor.

"Oh, yes," I said, "Um, you can, of course, sleep there. That will be your place. I will lay my head over there, near the doorway."

"Joseph," she said with a smile, "we are married now. I understand the angel told you not to know me until I have borne the child, but – can we not at least hold one another as we slumber? Besides, we must give every appearance of a normal couple, should someone enter unexpectedly."

I scratched at my neck. "Well, I – I suppose that would be appropriate. And you are right, I would rather not anyone ask why I refuse to lie with you.

But we must not dare do anything that would compromise the commandment I was given."

"Of course," she said. "If you feel any temptation at all, you must immediately distance yourself."

"Agreed."

I squatted down before her and took her hands in mine. Then I kissed her gently on the forehead. "Mary, I do love you."

"And I, you, my husband."

When I wasn't working on our house, Mary and I spent our time studying the scriptures together intently, striving to learn more about this mission – this great thing with which we had been entrusted. We stayed close to the spirit of God, obeying with exactness all the statutes and ordinances.

It was only a few weeks before Mary started to grow round in her belly, the Son of God extending her womb such that I could clearly see that she was with child.

Thankfully, our hasty marriage was timed along with her condition such that there would likely be no question of any impropriety having occurred. However, it was a possibility.

Mary must have known what I was thinking.

"Joseph, I would like to visit my cousin Elizabeth for while. I feel compelled to speak with her about her miraculous conception – and to offer my help to her as she brings forth a son into the world."

"Will you speak to her of – of what has

happened to us?"

"I do not know. Perhaps, if it feels right. After all, Gabriel told me of her conceiving. I feel it may be safe to share this secret with her. Joseph, I think I should leave soon, before anyone notices that I am with child."

"Yes," I said, "I think that would be best. If you are gone for a while, no one will give it much thought when you return appearing to be with child. They will not connect how far along you appear with the date of our wedding."

"You will accompany me?"

"I will travel with you, seeing you safely there. But then I will have to return to finish building our home, and to help my father. And to allow him to help me, as I set up my own carpentry shop."

"I understand. When shall we leave?"

"Let us leave tomorrow."

The next day, I packed one of my family's donkeys with some of Mary's belongings, and a few supplies for the journey, and we set off into the hill country of Judah to a tiny village called Ain Karem, which was next to the town of Mozah, situated near Jerusalem, where her cousin Elizabeth lived.

We arrived at the house of Zacharias and Elizabeth, a humble stone dwelling near the center of the town. Mary had told me that Zacharias, Elizabeth's husband, served a short distance away at the temple in Jerusalem. But he was home today, and greeted us at the door upon our arrival. Oddly, he said nothing; merely smiled and embraced Mary, and gestured for us to come in.

In the inner room, we found Elizabeth seated in

a chair in the corner. My first impression of her was that she was very old to be with child – but she looked nonetheless healthy and vibrant.

"Hello, Elizabeth!" Mary saluted warmly.

"Oh my," said Elizabeth in reply, placing her hand on her protruding belly. Her countenance suddenly seemed to take on the appearance of great joy, and she said, "The babe has leapt in my womb! Mary – oh, Mary! You truly are the most blessed of women – and the fruit of your womb is also so blessed! Tell me, why is it that I should be so favored as to receive a visit from the mother of the Lord?"

Mary and I looked at each other, at once confused and delighted.

How could Elizabeth possibly know of our secret? Had Gabriel told her also?

"Elizabeth, my soul is enlarged and made joyful by your greeting – and in my heart I magnify the Lord," said Mary, smiling through tears and stepping toward Elizabeth, taking her hand. She seemed to have an unspoken understanding with her cousin that even I could not quite grasp. "My spirit rejoices in God; for he has chosen me, a lowly virgin of Nazareth, and from this time forward all generations will call me blessed."

My wife was indeed blessed. And she was right – she would be known forever as the mother of the Messiah.

She continued, "Elizabeth, He that is mighty has done great things to me – things that I scarcely can understand. But I do know that He is forever merciful to those who honor Him. He is stronger than all, confounding those who think themselves wise. He brings all things into their proper order and loves all. And He will fulfill all His words."

These words of Mary struck me as very powerful – like a prophetess speaking. She had clearly absorbed much from our study of the scriptures – and she surely had an added measure of the Spirit about her now that she carried the Son of God. Her exultation and praise of God brought tears to my eyes, as well as the eyes of Elizabeth and Zacharias.

Zacharias stepped forward carrying a small writing tablet, onto which he quickly wrote something. I thought perhaps he was recording the words which Mary had spoken, but then he handed the tablet to Elizabeth.

"My husband wants to know how long you will be staying with us," said Elizabeth.

"Can he not speak?" I asked.

"No," said Elizabeth. "When the angel Gabriel announced to him in the temple that I would bring forth a son, being in my old age, and barren as well, Zacharias did not, at first, believe the angel. That he might learn to have greater faith, he has had his power of speech removed, that his doubting tongue may learn to believe before speaking. He has not uttered a word in nearly nine months."

I brought my hand toward my lips, suddenly relieved that I had believed Gabriel immediately.

"Will he regain his power of speech?" asked Mary.

"Yes," said Elizabeth, "the angel told him that when the prophecy had come to pass – that is, once I had given birth – the curse would be lifted."

"I see," I said. "I am sorry."

Zacharias wrote once again, and Elizabeth read. "Do not be sorry for me. I brought it upon myself, but it has done a great wonder in strengthening my faith. I feel blessed that this has happened."

"To answer your question," said Mary, "I would like, if possible, to stay until your child comes forth, and help you for a while afterward – about three months."

"Absolutely," said Elizabeth, "we welcome you to stay that long, and it would be very good to have you here to help me as the day draws near, and immediately after the child comes. And, your husband?"

"Joseph must return home for now – but he will come again to retrieve me." Mary put her hand to her mouth. "Oh, dear, I am so sorry – when our unborn children greeted each other, it caused me to be distracted, and I did not even introduce you! Mary, Zacharias – this is my husband Joseph – he who shall be the father of the Son of God."

CHAPTER IV – THE BIRTH OF JESUS

The days seemed to pass both slowly and quickly for me as I worked on our house with my father. Slowly because Mary did not come anymore, since she was with Elizabeth – and I missed her pleasant company and strong spirit.

Quickly because it seemed the time of the birth was approaching faster than I could accomplish my task. I worked hard six days a week to get the house done in time, the work days getting longer and longer so that I may have everything prepared for her return. I did not wish for us to remain at my father's house when she came back – while I appreciated the welcome of my family, it felt important that we have our own place in which to live once she brought forth the Messiah.

At last, the house was ready, and I returned to Ain Karem.

When I arrived, Elizabeth had given birth to a son they had named John, who was growing quickly – nearly three months old and very healthy. Seeing the babe gave me a swelling feeling in my heart. I was not sure if it was simply because it reminded me that there was soon to be a tiny baby boy in our own home, or something more – some special feeling from seeing he who would pave the way for the Messiah, according to the prophecies.

Zacharias could once again speak, his chastisement from the Lord lifted. He was in a jovial mood and it seemed as if being a father had made him younger than his many years. Fatherhood indeed suited the old man very well.

Mary was starting to become great with child, and it was so good to see her again. Following an evening meal and a good night's rest, we returned home.

Three months quickly passed, and the time drew near for Mary to give birth. I prepared our home in every possible way, trying to make it a place fit for a king, despite our humble circumstances. But before that great day could come, we received some troubling news.

"A census?" I asked my father.

"Yes," he said. "It seems Caesar Augustus is requiring each man to return to the city of his heritage to register for taxation for Rome. We must all comply – and we must all comply as soon as possible. We do not want to incur the wrath of the Empire – lately they have been seeking any excuse to seize property and exert their power in response to what they call non-compliance with their laws. We live peaceably with the Romans, but there has been some friction of late, and this latest Caesar is a greedy one."

It seemed as if we had only just returned from a journey to the south. Mary was due to give birth any day now. At least we would be in a company with my father's family, in case anything happened.

"Shall we not travel together, then?" I asked. "Bethlehem, the city of David, is also the city of your fathers."

"I cannot go immediately," my father said, "I must first accompany your mother's brother to their home city of Shechem for his accounting – he is old and ill, and will require assistance. We will follow soon after to Bethlehem. But this timing is actually good; by the time we reach Jerusalem, we will be in time to celebrate the Passover. You should start out now, as your journey will take longer, given Mary's condition."

"Very well," I said. "We will leave at once."

I looked at Mary, whose face showed me what she was thinking: she was not looking forward to another long journey on the back of a donkey. As large as she was now with child, surely all she wanted to do was lie down and rest. But she was ever faithful and dutiful.

"I will be ready to go in the morning," she said. "I just need to gather a few items for the trip. You never know how long these things can take."

As the sun rose, we were off. I felt disappointed that Mary had to leave the comfort and familiarity of our new home – and I struggled to suppress resentment for the Romans. I knew I should not feel that way in my heart – that it was a sin – so I pushed such thoughts away. But it was hard not to feel inconvenienced – to feel that it was not fair on my wife to be forced to make this additional journey, when all she really wanted was to get some much-deserved rest – especially after all the help she had given to her cousin Elizabeth, and making the long journey home only three months ago.

But before long, we were talking and laughing together as we went on our way – she always had the ability to put my mind at ease and forget my troubles. And what an example to me: if she could, in her condition, be in such good spirits, then surely I could.

Our donkey, a dark gray animal we'd had for several years, was well-laden with some bedclothes, a basket of food, three goatskins of water, and, of course, my wife. After six long days, with Mary feeling birthing pains for the last several miles, we reached Bethlehem.

The little city was quite crowded and bustling with many people – most of whom appeared to be travelers themselves, arriving to register for the tax. Even in the hills around the town, people had pitched tents. Animals were everywhere, along with many children.

"Joseph," said Mary, who was perched atop our donkey, "Joseph, I am so very tired and weary now. My back is hurting, and I do not feel I can go much further. I fear the babe should come tonight."

"I understand, Mary. We must find an inn. So far, they have all had signs hung out that say they are full. But I know there is one more, near the edge of the town. We are nearly there."

I felt very frustrated that there was nowhere for us to rest. All I wanted to do was provide a place for my wife in her time of need.

We finally reached the last inn. I knocked at the gate. There was the sound of a latch, and the gate creaked open.

"Hello?" said a wrinkled man with dark shoulder-length hair streaked with white. He glanced at Mary and back at me. "I'm truly sorry, but we just have no room."

"Wait, wait," I implored. "Please. My wife – look, she is great with child, and may even deliver this very night. Is there no place for us? Have you not even a very small spot where we may have some privacy and a place to lay our weary heads?"

"As I said, I am sorry – there is nothing. Every spot is occupied. You will have to go elsewhere."

"There *is* no other place! You are – were – our last hope."

I slowly turned, my head hanging low, and began to walk away.

Behind me, I heard a woman's voice murmuring with the innkeeper.

"Wait!" he cried out. "I've spoken with my wife. She suggests we offer you the small stable we have out back. It's not much, but it will be a roof over your heads, at least. There's hay you can lay on, and we'll bring you out some fresh water. Will that be acceptable?"

"Yes, yes," I said. "That will be all right – better than wandering the streets all night, or making our bed under the stars in a field. Thank you."

"Of course, you'll be sharing it with the animals."

"It is well," I said with a tired smile. "Perhaps they will be good company."

I led Mary, riding the donkey, around to the back of the inn, and across a small field to the stable. It was a low structure set into the side of a steep hill. Large timbers framed the front, with a small thatched roof covering the entrance. Within, the smells of livestock wafted thick on the evening air – cattle, horses, sheep, an ox, and a pair of donkeys making their home inside among the stacks of hay. I helped Mary down from our donkey, and she sat in the corner against the limestone wall on a soft pile of hay, sighing heavily as she lowered herself down, assisted by my hand.

I unpacked the donkey and arranged the bedclothes on the hay to make it more comfortable, and Mary laid back a little.

"Are you all right," I said, not really knowing how best to tend to her needs.

Before she could answer, the innkeeper's wife entered, carrying a large bucket of fresh water, and some additional bed clothes. "Just in case," she said, placing the bucket down and putting the extra bedclothes under Mary's head. "We don't have much, but if you need anything, please let me know. I just feel so awful that you must be out here."

"Do not feel bad," Mary said. "It is far better than having no shelter. The evening is growing cool – it will be good to have this place to rest."

The innkeeper's wife left us alone. I knelt next to Mary. "I'm sorry, Mary. This is hardly the way you should have to spend the night."

"Joseph, the pains are getting closer together. I think it will be tonight."

"The – the birth? You think you will deliver –

tonight? *Here?"*

Mary nodded, then I saw her face clench a little in pain.

"Mary, I have – I have never delivered a baby – I've not even *seen* a baby delivered. I do not know what to do."

"I was there for my cousin Elizabeth," said Mary, after taking a long, slow breath. "I saw what the midwife did. I will tell you what to do. You can do this, Joseph."

I stepped to the doorway and looked out across the field, then up to the black sky, speckled with thousands of tiny stars. I closed my eyes and said a silent prayer into those vast heavens, asking God to help me – to help Mary. And to forgive me for being responsible for the ignominy of the Messiah being born in a lowly cattle stall.

A cool breeze whipped at my face. I opened my watering eyes, and stared at the stars once more. Then I craned my neck to see the stars overhead.

And I saw it.

Directly overhead, the brightest, most amazing star I had ever seen.

It felt like a sign – like comfort from God, just for me – to let me know that it was going to be all right. That somehow this situation was all part of His plan.

I blinked away the tears and returned to Mary's side.

"It will be all right," I said. "What is the first thing I need to do?"

Mary smiled, as if she had somehow known all along what I had just realized: that everything was proceeding according to God's will. "We will need a fire, and some clean, warm water," she said. "A clean blade. Salt. And the swaddling strips that I brought in our pack."

"And then?"

"And then we wait. And you hold my hand," she added, not reflecting any of the worry that I still felt quivering deep in my belly.

I nodded and got to work, building a small fire in the corner, up against the limestone wall as far from the hay as possible for safety. I found a clay vessel and started some water boiling, found the swaddling clothes and salt in Mary's pack, and retrieved my blade from my pack, ensuring it was sharp and clean.

"Are you hungry?" I asked. "Would you like some bread?"

Mary was clearly in pain again, and simply shook her head, her hands forming fists as she resisted crying out.

I knelt and held her hand, and we waited for the next wave of pain, which came only a few moments later. She tightened her grip on my hand, surprising me with her strength.

"Joseph, I think he will be here very soon. Bring the water."

I retrieved the water, which was already boiling, and placed it nearby. "What else – what next?"

"Oh," she said, breathing heavily. "Oh! Next, you will have to – you will have to deliver the baby."

I swallowed hard. Although we were husband and wife, I felt very nervous about this. But I also knew that I must do whatever it took to make sure the Messiah entered the world safely. "Very well,"

I said. "I am ready."

I will never forget the moments that followed. Despite the obvious pain, Mary quietly stayed steadfast, making almost no sound as she brought forth the babe with several intense pushes. Tears filled my eyes as he came into my rough hands – this perfect, sweet, innocent child. I could scarcely believe that I was the first to behold the Messiah in the flesh – the first to hold him.

He did not cry – only made a few soft gurgling sounds.

I used the sharp blade to cut the fleshy cord that attached him to his mother, and followed Mary's instruction to stop the bleeding, then handed this precious child to Mary. Together, we used a cloth and the now-cooled water to wash the babe, then carefully rubbed his skin with the salt to thoroughly cleanse him. Then, gently, I helped Mary wrap Jesus in the swaddling clothes, which consisted of several long strips of cloth, until he was snugly bound and ready to rest in his mother's arms.

Jesus had arrived.

CHAPTER V – UNEXPECTED VISITORS

The night seemed to go quickly, as Mary alternately nursed and then held the sleeping Jesus. I kept her fed and comfortable, as best I could, given the conditions. Finally, she was so tired, I took the babe in my arms and she slept. Then I got tired, too, and laid down beside her for a few minutes, but as I started to fall asleep, I worried I would hurt the child, so I carefully prepared a soft place in a feeding trough and laid the sleeping Jesus down to sleep. I could hardly believe I was placing the Messiah in a manger, but it was the best location available.

I stepped to the doorway and looked out. The star overhead continued to shine brightly like a beacon to the world. That world was very, very quiet at this late hour – not a soul stirred for what seemed like miles around. Not even a breeze blew – it was truly *silent*. Satisfied that we were safe, I returned to Mary's side and, listening to her breathe, and the baby breathe, slipped into a deep slumber.

What seemed like a very short time later, I awoke to the sound of footsteps. My heart pounded. Who could be here? I quickly comforted myself when I realized it must be the kindly innkeeper's wife coming to check on us.

Within the stable, it had grown quite dark, as the fire had died down to a barely-glowing pile of embers. Although it was deep in the night, the sky outside the doorway glowed a faint indigo-blue because of the bright star overhead. Someone stepped to the doorway. And then another, and another. This was not the innkeeper's wife, as I had anticipated.

I sat up straight, my heart thumping in my chest.

"Hail," said a man's voice. He did not sound dangerous – he sounded nervous.

I stood and approached the doorway, so as not to have to call out and wake Mary or the child. "Greetings," I said. I saw that the speaker was dressed as a shepherd and carried a shepherd's crook. His companions – several men and boys, were likewise attired. "I'm sorry," I said, "this stable is occupied this night. We are here with the innkeeper's permission. You will have to find shelter elsewhere."

"Is this the place – the place where the Savior who is Christ the Lord is born this night? We have come to worship him."

I was completely surprised. Nobody knew we were here. And certainly nobody but Mary and I knew that the babe in the manger was the Son of God. The birth had been quiet; no messengers had been sent out from here to announce it.

Messengers!

"Tell me," I said, "how did you know?"

"May we come in?"

"Yes," I said. They seemed harmless, and humble, and they said they were here to worship, so I allowed them to enter.

When we came in to the back part of the stable, Mary was awake. I stoked the coals and added some wood that we might have more warmth and light.

"Mary, we have visitors. They say they are here to worship Jesus."

Mary's reaction was the same as mine. "How did you know?" she asked them.

The men knelt on the ground and bowed reverently to Mary and to the babe in the manger, who slept on in peace.

"We were abiding in our field toward the hill country south and west of this place. We were doing that which we do every night – keeping watch over our flock. And the angel of the Lord came upon us, and the glory of the Lord shone round about us."

Another – a young man of about twelve years of age, interjected. "We were very afraid. The angel was glorious and terrifying."

The first shepherd continued. "But the angel said to us, 'Do not fear; for I bring you good tidings of great joy, which will be to all people. For unto you is born this day in the city of David a Savior, who is Christ the Lord. And this will be a sign to you; You will find the babe wrapped in swaddling clothes, lying in a manger.'"

The man nodded toward the child, who, lying in the manger, wrapped in swaddling clothes, fulfilled this announcement by the angel.

Now a third man spoke. "After the angel said that, there was suddenly with that angel a multitude of the heavenly host praising God, and saying, 'Glory to God in the highest, and on earth peace, good will toward men.' They sang a song of love and joy so powerful, it nearly overcame us." Tears filled his eyes. "It was the most amazing thing we have ever seen."

The first man completed the story, "After the angels left us and returned into the heavens, we said to each other, 'Let us go now to Bethlehem, and see this thing which has come to pass, which the Lord has made known unto us.' And we came here with great haste, being led by the star which shines brightly above this very stable – and by a feeling inside that seemed to guide us directly here. And here we are. We apologize for intruding on your privacy – but, after all, we were led here by God."

I looked at Mary. "It's all right," I said. "We are just very tired – and of course, I am very protective of the child. But we are pleased that the Lord has made this thing known unto you, that you may worship the Messiah."

"And, to be honest," said Mary with a small smile, "it is somewhat of a relief to finally be able to share our secret."

I nodded. "Yes, until now, nobody else has known of this miraculous thing. It pleases us to share this now with you humble shepherds, whom God has chosen to be witnesses."

I then lifted the newborn babe from the manger and presented him to the shepherds. "Behold," I said, "His name is Jesus."

The shepherds stared in reverent awe for a few silent moments.

"We will be honored to share these great tidings with the world," said the oldest of the shepherds, who wore a long white beard. "Come, let us go into Bethlehem and all the land round about, and make known this wondrous news!"

"Thank you so much for allowing us to see the Christ child," said another of the shepherds as they began to depart. "I will remember this throughout my whole life."

The last of them exited the doorway, bowing as he left, and we were once again left in a still, peaceful night. Mary laid back down and seemed to be asleep again almost instantly – she was so fatigued.

I checked on the babe, who continued to sleep in the manger, seeming to be perfectly content in his humble bed of hay. He was magnificent. I was suddenly overcome with awe, and dropped to my knees and worshipped him, tears streaming down my face.

I pondered the events of the day, including what the shepherds had said about spreading the news of his birth. I thought deeply on these things – what would become of us – of our little family – now that everyone knew? Would we be able to raise Jesus with any amount of peace, or would the world flock to our home in an endless stream of worshippers? What was expected of us – by God, and by man?

As I contemplated the enormity of it all, I laid down in the hay and fell asleep beside my wife, exhausted from the most amazing day of my life.

CHAPTER VI – INFANCY

For a while, we received no visitors to the stable. On the third day, the innkeeper's wife came and let us know that some space had become available at the inn – news that was very welcome, as a cattle stall was no place for a new mother and child. The weather was not harsh, and Mary and Jesus were well, but I felt bad that the conditions were so dirty and uncomfortable. It was my job to keep my family safe and healthy, and provide for all their needs. Being stuck out in the stable made me feel inadequate as a husband and father, even though I understood the circumstances were beyond my immediate control. Moving into the inn helped relieve that burden of guilt on my shoulders.

The inn, it turned out, was not much of an improvement.

There were fewer animals nearby, but there were many more people – which meant less privacy. However, it was good to be closer to where we could get food and water, and the innkeeper's wife provided a fresh set of bedclothes.

When I wasn't tending to the needs of Mary and the babe, I spent my time staring out of our little alcove at the rest of the inn, which comprised a large rectangular area with many alcoves like our own all facing the center, and the travelers' animals kept in the middle area. The innkeeper's wife had prepared a drapery that could be drawn across the front of our alcove to offer a small amount of privacy, but there was so much noise – it was a wonder Jesus slept at all.

Being springtime, with the weather inconsistent, the fourth and fifth night were quite colder outside than the first few, so I was glad for the warm comforts of the inn, despite the noise and other discomforts.

By the sixth day, it was time to set out for Jerusalem. To fulfill tradition, Jesus needed to be circumcised on the eighth day, and my father knew a good mohel in Jerusalem who could do it for us. Also, my father and his family were now staying there, so we would have a place to stay, and he could introduce us to the rabbi who would serve as mohel.

The journey from Bethlehem to Jerusalem was not long, but it was not any easier to traverse the distance with a newborn and convalescing mother than it was with a woman great with child and anticipating giving birth. In fact, it was much more difficult, since I was now responsible for not only a woman, but a woman and a vulnerable newborn. And not just any newborn – the Messiah himself.

We stopped several times to rest, and so Mary could nurse the precious infant. Finally, by the evening of Jesus' seventh day, we arrived in the great walled city of Jerusalem and found the lodgings where my father's family was staying.

The building was a brown, stone, two-story structure attached to a row of other homes. Father had said it belonged to his uncle's friend. Thankfully, it was only a short walk from the temple. I tied up our donkey, and we escaped the hot sunshine as we entered and found my family seated to an evening meal.

"It is good to see you, son," said Father, standing and embracing me warmly. "Hello, Mary. Ah, and here is the babe! Let me see my grandson!"

"Hello, Father," I said, as Mary handed the infant to him. As Father held Jesus, we greeted my mother and siblings, who also desired to see our new child.

Along the way from Bethlehem, Mary and I had discussed sharing our secret with the family. Since the angels had announced it to the shepherds, and the shepherds had gone forth and proclaimed the news to – to whomever they had met that night – we decided we should be the ones to share the truth with our families, since they were bound to get word of it somehow, and it seemed best that it come directly from us.

Father invited us to sit to meal with them, which we were glad to do, as we were tired and hungry from our journey.

"Father," I said, as we finished eating, "there is something of immense importance that Mary and I need to tell you. To tell the whole family."

"Yes?" Father encouraged me, before taking a sip of his water. "What is it?"

I looked at Mary, as if to make sure she hadn't changed her mind. She nodded almost imperceptibly. I took a deep breath and proceeded.

"Father, have you heard any word being spread among the people – about the Messiah being born?"

"Actually, yes," said Father. "We have heard a rumor – people are saying that a week ago, in Bethlehem, a child was born who is the King of Kings. If true, it is the greatest news of my lifetime! But, somehow, I doubt it. Why would the Messiah be born – as it was said in this story – in a stable?"

I breathed heavily once again, and felt the sweat starting to form on my brow. I swallowed hard, and said, "Father, I am not certain why the Messiah was born in such humble conditions. To such humble servants of God. But I suppose it was, at least in part, because there was no room for us at the inn."

"No room for you? For you – what, what are you saying, son? Joseph – are you saying that – that this child – that your son is the Messiah?"

I nodded.

It seemed that the whole family gasped in unison. Father had a look of bewilderment on his face, but he did not look angry. For some reason I had expected him to be angry, because I expected him to think I was not being truthful. But his face changed from surprise, to one of wonderment and then to one of joy.

"I see that it is true," he said. "I can feel it – in my heart." He beamed. "Let me look once more upon the child – upon the Messiah!"

Mary placed the babe in Father's arms once

more. The whole family gathered round and stared down at the boy.

"He is magnificent!" Father whispered. A tear came to his eye. "How – tell us – how do you know he is the Messiah?"

Mary and I related the whole story, from Gabriel's visit to each of us, the reason for our hasty wedding, the visit to Elizabeth and Zacharias, and even the visit of the shepherds.

"I'm sorry," I said, "for not telling you sooner. It just didn't feel right. I did not want to do anything contrary to that which we had been commanded by the angel. He did not tell us not to tell anyone, but there was a strong feeling that we should not share that sacred experience and knowledge until the time was right. And now, the time felt right."

"Besides," added Mary, "we would rather you heard it from us than hear it from some stranger as a rumor, and perhaps not receive the true story."

Father just nodded, and continued to look upon the infant in his arms.

"You are fatigued from your trip," he finally said, "you should get some rest."

We agreed, and went to sleep early. Jesus slept well, only waking three times for nursing, and in the morning we headed to the temple, feeling refreshed.

The next day, according to tradition and to keep the commandments, Jesus was circumcised by Father's rabbi friend who was a mohel.

Rather than make the long trek back to Nazareth, we decided to stay at that home in Jerusalem for the next few weeks. On the fortieth day, it was time to go to the temple.

Mary and I both felt strongly impressed to present Jesus at the temple, since it was, after all, God's house – and he was God's son – and it was also a part of our tradition. Together with my father and his family, we went up to the temple, a grand stone edifice of glory and majesty that seemed to take up a huge portion of Jerusalem all on its own, when you included the outer walls. It was quite busy, with many faithful people attending to the various tasks and rituals common to the holy place.

Lacking money for a lamb, we purchased two turtledoves for the sacrifice. Shortly afterward, an elderly man approached us – he seemed very interested in us and the baby.

"Greetings," he said with a smile. "I am Simeon. And this," he said, gesturing to an aged woman who stepped up alongside him, "is Anna."

"Hello," I said.

"Are you Joseph?"

"Yes," I said hesitantly. I did not know this man. How did he know me?

"The Holy Ghost has led me to you," he said, as if answering my unspoken question. "Many years have I waited for this day." He smiled broadly, truly exuding joy.

"I do not understand," I said, glancing over to Mary, who held Jesus close.

"Long ago, it was revealed to me by the Holy Ghost that I should not see death before I had seen the Messiah. I came by the Spirit here into the temple, and when I saw you bring in the child, I knew – I knew it was him of whom the prophets have testified. May I take him up into my arms and bless him?"

I looked at Mary, and she seemed very much at ease with this. She looked to me for confirmation, and I nodded. She handed Simeon the babe.

Simeon smiled again, his eyes closed, and said, "Blessed be the name of God! Lord, now let your servant depart in peace, according to your word, for my eyes have seen your salvation, which you have prepared before the face of all people; a light to lighten the Gentiles, and the glory of your people Israel."

Mary and I looked at each other. Was this how it was going to be? Wise old men speaking grand things of the baby, everywhere we went? I looked back at Simeon, and tears streamed down his face. He handed Jesus back to Mary, thanking her for the privilege.

Then Simeon blessed us, and said to Mary, "This child is set for the fall and rising again of many in Israel; and for a sign that will be spoken against – and a sword will pierce through your own soul also – that the thoughts of many hearts may be revealed."

My father took me aside and whispered to me. "Joseph, this man confirms those things which I felt in my heart when you told me of Jesus. An additional witness to make strong my knowledge of the Savior! Perhaps he will witness likewise to others."

"Perhaps," I said, still taken aback by Simeon's words of prophecy.

Then the old woman spoke to us. "As Simeon said, my name is Anna, and I am known as a prophetess. I am the daughter of Phanuel, of the tribe of Asher. I have been a widow now for eighty years, and have served in the temple all this time since I lost my husband, praying and fasting both day and night. I thank God that I have lived to see this day, that the Savior of the World has come into the world, and into this temple. Today is a great day for all in Israel who look for redemption!"

It warmed my heart that God had made known to these two faithful servants that Jesus was the Christ, the very son of the living God. That they got the chance to look upon him with their eyes before leaving this life. How kind and loving is our God!

The next day, we packed up our things and headed out on the long journey back to Nazareth. It was going to be nice to be able to finally move into our new home, and to be a family.

CHAPTER VII – A HASTY ESCAPE

The next two years, life in Nazareth seemed very normal – like any other young family. No more blessings from aged wise men or women in the temple, and not much talk of the true nature of our little boy.

He was amazing, though. He was always obedient – a perfect child. Jesus learned faster than other children, and shortly after he could walk, he was learning words – and soon was praying like no child I'd ever heard of – filling our home with the spirit of God.

But as the days turned to weeks, and the weeks to months, we got settled into our life. He was our little boy, and all we knew; so our life, naturally, started to feel normal – since it was simply our life. We studied the scriptures diligently, and prayed for guidance, but we received no heavenly messengers, and time marched on without incident.

At first, the only thing that really served as a powerful, visible reminder of our mission was the new star that hung high overhead each night, burning brightly as a clear sign to us that our life was really anything but normal. Still, even the new star was something that one could get used to after long enough.

One day, after a long hard day framing a new home on the east side of Nazareth, we had just finished our evening meal when an impressive caravan of visitors approached, crossing the south end of my father's property and arriving at our home.

The visitors' company included at least a dozen camels, several pack animals, and a small contingent of servants, some of whom were armed with scimitars, but appeared unthreatening. But the most impressive were the five royal-looking men who sat atop the lead camels.

Each wore princely robes – red, gold, purple, with fine embroidery – and majestic headwear. Two of them appeared to be from the Far East (as I had met such men once before, in Jerusalem), and the other three were dark-skinned. Each had a differently-styled beard. All looked serene and powerful and intelligent.

I went out to greet them.

"Hail, travelers, what brings you to my humble home?"

Each of the five leaders dismounted from their camels and approached me. I don't know why, but something about their regal nature inspired me to bow to them out of respect, almost without thinking.

"I am Melchyor," said one of the dark ones in a rich, deep voice. He spoke quite passable Aramaic for a foreigner – obviously a learned man. His kind-looking eyes glanced overhead toward *our* star, for just a moment, then he asked, "Is this the home of he was born King of the Jews?"

I was more than a little startled by this question. Outside of my family, we'd not heard of this kind of reference to Jesus in nearly two years. Some instinctive, protective part of me made my stomach clench as I tingled with tension. Cautiously, I asked, "You have told me your name, but who are you?"

Melchyor gestured to his companions. "These great men who accompany me are named Caspar, Balthazar, Rentha, and Denji. We are kings of our own lands, and have traveled thousands of miles on our pilgrimage. We have studied the ancient prophets, surveyed the heavens, tracked the stars, and seen great visions from God. He has led us here, to this very location, under the Great Star of David, as we have called it these past two years."

"And why are you here?" I asked, still apprehensive.

"Why, to worship the Son of God, of course," said Melchyor with a smile that showed his bright white teeth. "We come bearing gifts for the long-promised Messiah."

I released my breath and relaxed my muscles. A feeling of comfort came over me, and I smiled back. "In that case, welcome to my home. I am Joseph. Please, direct your servants to the back, where they can take care of the animals. You may come in and sup with Mary and I, and of course see the child."

The five dignified travelers followed me into the house. Mary looked up in surprise at the invading group. I quickly assuaged her concerns. "Mary, these honored guests have come from afar to see Jesus – to worship him. They've been traveling since – how long have you been traveling?" I turned and asked Melchyor.

"Two years," he said simply in his rich voice. "Since the star first appeared, to guide our way. We are not Jews, but we have our own sacred writings – we knew the sign would come; we only needed to know the direction. Once it came, we were ready. We left joyfully, and have now arrived with greater joy."

Mary stood, "Well, I'll get Jesus, so that your joy may be full." At that moment, Jesus came shuffling in from the back room. "Ah, here he is now. Jesus, there are some men here to meet you."

The little boy ran to his mother and into her arms. The five wise men each fell to bended knee and bowed their heads reverently.

"We are honored to be here in your presence," said the one called Balthazar. "We are kings on this earth – but you – you are *our* king. We have gifts for you – tokens of our devotion." He reached into his robes and produced a small flask of crushed brown crystals. "Olibanum."

"Incense?" I asked.

"Yes," said Balthazar, "the very finest. May your home always be filled with the warm and comforting aroma reminiscent of your temple at Jerusalem."

"Thank you," I said, taking the flask in behalf of Jesus.

Next, the one called Caspar stepped forward and presented a small, ornately-inscribed box that appeared to be made of copper; it was small enough to fit in his hand. "And this contains myrrh," he said. "The precious resin is most prized in my country – use it in good health."

I took it with a nod of gratitude.

Then Rentha, Denji, and Melchyor stepped outside for a moment and returned carrying a heavy-looking chest. "This," said Melchyor, opening the lid, revealing a glistening material, "contains gold. It is mostly in the coinage of our respective nations, but it has great worth no matter where you use it. May your family never want for the essentials of life."

The abundant amount of gold was breathtaking. "Thank you," I said, "but how can we accept such a gift? It does not feel right."

"Please," said Melchyor, "we have come such a long way to offer these gifts. They are precious to us, but not nearly as precious as this opportunity to see the Messiah. Besides, you may need it sooner than you think."

I was curious what he meant by that, but remembered my manners and asked the five weary travelers to partake of some food and drink.

We washed, and sat to eat. I asked Melchyor, "What did you mean – that we may need that gold soon?"

Melchyor looked at his companions, and took a sip of juice, then spoke in a low voice. "On our way here, we stopped at Jerusalem. We had an audience with Herod, the man who calls himself king of this land. We asked him where we may find he that is born King of the Jews, for we had seen his star in the east, and were seeking him that we might worship him. He did not answer us at first, but he called a counsel of his chief priests and scribes, and a short time later informed us that we should look in Bethlehem. We spoke to some shepherds there who directed us here to Nazareth."

Balthazar took over the story. "When we left Herod at Jerusalem, he told us to report to him where exactly the babe could be found, that he might worship him also. But just last night, each of us had a similar dream, in which God warned us not to return by way of Jerusalem – that we should not report the location of Jesus to Herod. This can only mean that Herod does not mean to worship Jesus. We think he is a jealous man, who craves power and fears the loss of it."

"So," continued Melchyor, "we will depart to our own country a different way. But, should you have any – unusual – needs, the gold may become quite useful to you."

"I understand," I said. "Thank you."

Mary looked at me, and I could see the concern on her face as she held Jesus close. Jesus, who had been listening intently, seemed to perceive Mary's worry, and gently stroked the back of her head.

Whatever happened, I would make sure my family was safe. Whatever it took.

I stood and walked to our outer doorway, my mind racing. Could there really be danger? How could anyone want to hurt our little boy – how could anyone even consider harming the Son of

God?

I looked out and saw that the caravan of the kings had already set up several tents on my property, and the servants were bedding down for the night. I looked directly overhead at the star once more, then returned to our guests.

"We will leave at first light," said Rentha. "Thank you for this opportunity. Jesus is wonderful – a perfect child. It has been an honor we shall never forget."

The five kings departed to their tents, and Mary, Jesus and I all went to sleep soon afterward. It was hard to get to sleep at first, as I was anxious regarding this news of Herod brought to us by the wise men. But before long, I found myself asleep.

But it was no ordinary sleep.

As I slumbered, I felt a feeling I had not felt in nearly three years. My mind seemed to wake up – to be thinking clearly, to be in control – but I knew I was still asleep.

And then I saw him – the bright, glorious angel, Gabriel.

"Hail, Joseph," he said, his voice penetrating to my heart.

"Gabriel. Am I asleep?"

"Yes. But I am real." Although kind, his face was not full of joy, as it had been when he announced to me that Jesus was going to be born. He seemed concerned – serious. "I have been sent to warn you. The wise kings who spoke to you this night – they are correct. Herod does not mean to worship the child – he means to destroy him. And he will find you and Mary and Jesus if you remain in this land – it will only be a matter of time.

Therefore, arise, and take the young child and his mother, and flee into Egypt, and remain there until I bring you word."

Gabriel vanished from before my sight, the vision closed, and I awoke with a start. My heart pounding, I roused Mary and whispered, "Mary, we must gather our things and leave. Immediately."

"What? Leave?" she said groggily. "Now? Where? What is wrong?"

"I have had a visit from our angel."

"Gabriel?"

"Yes. God wants us to flee this very night."

"Where?"

"To Egypt."

Mary looked stunned. For a moment, she looked like she would cry, but her emotion quickly turned to one of resolve. "I'll get Jesus and pack the food."

"I'll gather the other supplies and prepare the animals. I think we'll need three, to pack all that we'll need. Including the gold."

In a rush of breathless packing and preparing, we were ready to leave within two hours. The night was still pitch dark, save the light of our star. I made a brief visit to my father's house, awoke him and mother, and told them all, then returned to my own house to collect Mary and Jesus.

On our way out, we awoke the kings in their tents and thanked them, then, under cover of darkness, we left everything behind. Despite it being the middle of the night, my heart beat hard, and my mind was active and alert. My number one concern was the safety of my family.

Gabriel had said Herod – the king – intended to *destroy* Jesus. This perfect little child – the Son of God.

Destroy him.

I had no idea how long we would have to spend in Egypt – a place I had never been – but right now it did not matter. As long as we were following the commandment of God, I knew we would be safe.

CHAPTER VIII – LIFE AMONG THE PYRAMIDS

We'd managed to make it several miles out of Nazareth by the time dawn made the hills to the east stand out in silhouette against the brightening sky. The road was very quiet – really no people anywhere at this early hour – but I couldn't help constantly looking over my shoulder as we went. It felt like Herod's men were hiding behind every rock, ready to spring on my little family.

I gripped my staff tightly and looked over at Mary, who rode one of our donkeys, with the sleeping Jesus in her arms.

He was getting so big.

I wondered if, somehow, he understood all this – perhaps even better than we did.

All I knew was that I would not feel any comfort until we were well beyond the southern borders of Judea – and that would not be for another few days of hasty journeying.

We pitched our tent for the first two days of the

journey, and ate the provisions we had brought with us. On the third day, as we approached a point in the road where we could either go forward through Jerusalem, or work our way around to the west and avoid the city, we had a decision to make.

"Mary," I said, as we stopped and drank some water from one of the goat skin vessels hanging from the second donkey in our three-animal caravan, "Jerusalem will be a good location to purchase some additional supplies for our journey southward. We may also be able to purchase an additional animal to carry the supplies – we will need plenty for this very long trip."

"It would also be nice to visit the temple one last time – it may be a long time before we can worship there again," she said.

"I had the same thought myself," I said. "But I am concerned for our safety. If Herod is looking for us, I am sure he would have his men searching in Jerusalem. We would be better off sticking to the less traveled roads, and avoiding the city altogether. But we need the provisions."

"We could get the provisions in Hebron," Mary suggested.

"Yes, I nodded. Perhaps that is best. Let us go to the right, then. It is more hilly, and a longer route, but I think it will be worth it."

Our little family, with our animals, turned right and headed up the slope toward the hills. A few miles later, we could see Jerusalem in the distance to the east – we were passing the great city.

Then I heard Mary sniffing. She was quietly crying.

I stopped walking. "Mary, what is it? Are you

all right?"

She nodded. "Yes, I am well enough. I am just saddened that we will not see the temple again – for an unknown time. And then I started thinking about home. We will not see your family, or my family, or anyone in Nazareth, either. We are in exile."

I didn't know what to say. She was absolutely right.

I put my arm around her. "Mary, it will be all right. We are doing God's will. He will take care of us. And I know we will return, because the angel said he would call for us at the appointed time."

Mary wiped away her tears and took a deep breath, then looked ahead steadfastly, and said, "Yes – that is true. Let's keep moving."

For his part, Jesus seemed to be doing quite well with the journey, taking it all in stride. He ate, he slept, he walked – though he mostly rode the donkey – or sometimes my shoulders. He never complained.

Later that evening, as we began to drop down out of the hills into the vicinity of Hebron, we encountered another family on the road, approaching from the opposite direction. As we got closer, I could see that they were stopped, and seemed to be in some distress.

Their caravan consisted of six donkeys and two oxen, along with what appeared to be at least six children – four of whom looked to be under eight years old, some of them crying. The mother of the family leaned over the father, who lay alongside the road on some bedclothes.

"Hail," I said as we neared. "Are you in need of

assistance?"

The woman looked up at me, and tears filled her eyes. "My husband – he is suddenly taken with a fever. He can barely move, and cannot speak. Night is falling – I do not know what to do."

Mary immediately dug into one of our packs and pulled out the myrrh. "Here, place some of this balm on his tongue; it will help until we can get him to a physician."

As soon as he was administered to, I helped the woman quickly set up two of her tents a few paces from the side of the road. I then set up our tent for Mary and Jesus, and returned to the woman and her fevered husband. I lifted the man up off the ground, and placed him on one of our donkeys, laying him face down and cross-ways, since he had no strength to sit up.

"I'll take your husband to Hebron and find a physician as quickly as possible. I'll make sure he is taken care of – Mary will stay here with you. In the morning, we will return and help you break camp and help you with anything else you need."

The woman fell to her knees, "Oh, thank you, thank you!"

The man moaned, and I left quickly, fearing for his life.

As I moved as quickly as possible down the road, I also feared to be leaving Mary and Jesus alone. Was this stranger's life more important than theirs? More important than the safety and well-being of the Messiah? Was this detour violating God's command to flee directly to Egypt?

As these thoughts swirled around my head, I looked at the face of the sick man. He was clearly suffering. A new thought entered my mind and heart – clear and comforting and reassuring. It seemed to say, *you are doing the right thing – it is not wrong to serve your neighbor – your own family will be safe, and you will be blessed.*

Feeling a sense of peace, I concentrated on the task at hand: to find the nearest doctor in Hebron. As we got near the city, night enveloped us – the only light coming from the moon and stars, and the few homes that were still burning lamps within, creating a soft glow that indicated the city was in front of us. When we reached the first house, I knocked upon the door. After several moments, a long-bearded man answered.

"Yes?"

I gestured to the patient draped across the donkey's back. "This man is very ill. Can you please tell me how to get to the nearest physician?"

"Oh, yes," said the man. "Turn left at the end of this road, fourth home on the right. His name is Anathas."

'Thank you."

I hurried on, following the directions, and arrived at the house. The doctor appeared to have already been asleep, but he quickly snapped into action when he saw the sick man. I stayed while he administered to him. Once the man seemed to be doing better, and was sleeping, I reached into a pocket in my robes for my purse, and pulled out several of the gold coins the wise men had given us, and offered to pay the physician well for his services.

He peered curiously at the foreign coins, but did not turn it down.

I paid him to keep the man there overnight, then returned to my family and his.

By the time I got there, it was false dawn, but nobody was stirring. I laid down in our tent next to Mary and Jesus, and fell into a deep sleep.

As the sun appeared in the east, we all arose, packed up camp, and we all returned once more to Hebron, where I reunited the woman and her family with their husband and father. The man was doing much better.

"We do not know how to thank you," he said as he held his wife.

"No need," I said. "We hope the remainder of your journey is better than the first part."

With that, we left the doctor's house, and made our way into the main market area of Hebron to purchase more supplies and animals for the long desert journey ahead.

At one street seller of pack animals, I offered a handful of the gold coins in exchange for three additional donkeys. The hairy, dark-eyed man stared suspiciously at the money.

"It's legitimate," I said nervously. I held my breath as he continued to turn the coins over in his hand, looking at them closely.

"I can see for myself that this is real gold," he said gruffly. "I am just wondering how a poor Jew came to be in possession of this exotic denomination."

"Uh, I received it from some travelers," I said. "Foreign men."

"In exchange for what?" he asked with a growl.

I stood a little taller as I considered the real meaning of the exchange that had been made back at my home. "That's none of your concern," I said. "Do we have a bargain, or do I take my business elsewhere?"

The man shook his head wearily and pocketed the money. "Yes. Take the donkeys and leave."

I breathed a sigh of relief, and we continued southward across the city. We reached a market, where I used a few more of the gold to obtain a fair amount of food, six more goatskins of water, and another tent (I wanted to be sure we would always have shelter). I also purchased a bow with arrows, in case I ended up having to hunt for food. I was not very practiced at hunting, but I had basic skills enough to be confident I could kill and dress an animal if the need arose. Thankfully, my father had taught me when I was young.

I missed my father. It had not been that long since we left, but just knowing that it could be a very long time until we returned made me miss my family that much more.

I packed up the new animals with our additional equipment, keeping a wary eye out for any man who may be one of Herod's killers. Everyone looked like they might be one of Herod's killers. We carried on with our journey, and I was glad to see the city behind us.

As we got several miles south of Hebron, the land flattened out and became much more barren. That night, the wind picked up fiercely, which made it very difficult to set up our tent, and the animals were not particularly happy to have no way of avoiding the strong gusts that blew all night. At one point, I feared our tent would blow away before I had it properly staked.

I slept little that night, concerned for the well-being of Mary and Jesus. Mary slept on and off, and Jesus slumbered with no apparent trouble at all.

In the morning, in addition to taking down the tent and packing up, I had to spend some time collecting several of our items which had blown right away from where the donkeys were tied and tumbled to the east – some quite far away. Thankfully, the wind had died back down by that time, and I was able to round up our belongings without too much trouble.

We moved on, traveling in a south and west direction for several more days. The land grew more and more arid – truly a desert – and the wind at night was constant. I learned quickly to tie down our belongings tightly before going to sleep.

One night, our belongings remained intact, but the tent itself was ripped to shreds by the bellowing gusts. By morning, it was useless – damaged beyond repair. We left the tattered material behind, and I realized I had been prompted by God to purchase that second tent back in Hebron, for we would surely need it.

We saw few villages along the way, but those we did find afforded us the opportunity to purchase additional provisions, so that I didn't need to hunt. This was good, since we did not see many wild beasts in this wilderness – certainly nothing that looked edible.

Finally, we reached the borders of Egypt. Now we needed to determine where we would stay.

It was strange, as we traveled from village to village the first few days, to find no Jews at all. It was not critical that we find a place with Jews, but it seemed like it would be to our benefit to be among our own people. We did not meet outright hostility in these eastern Egyptian towns, but most of the people gave us the "no room at the inn" story – only it seemed not to ring true, as the places were not particularly crowded. Most suggested we go on to Alexandria, where we would find many more people of our own kind.

Alexandria, we were told, was another three days' journey across the Nile Delta. I did not want my family to have to wander from town to town like vagabonds, so I prayed about it. After some time meditating on the question, I felt impressed that we should indeed go all the way to Alexandria, and thus we did.

Upon arrival at the huge port city on the Mediterranean, we were directed to a part of the city inhabited almost exclusively by a large number of Jews, called the Shamar.

The district appeared to be at least ten times larger than Nazareth. A teeming, vibrant Jewish community, the area seemed as though it were set apart from the rest of the Egyptian city – like a little piece of Judea in the midst of another very different world.

As I led our little caravan down a narrow dirt street lined with tightly-packed white-walled buildings, I was startled by a hand laid on my shoulder. I spun around.

"Are you Joseph?"

My body stiffened, a fiery tingle shot to all my limbs as fear flooded my veins and I looked immediately to Mary and Jesus, wary for their safety.

"Who is asking?"

The man smiled. "My name is Amnun." He leaned in and whispered, "I can help you. Please, come with me to my home – I will explain everything."

I stared into his deep brown eyes for a few moments, then started to relax my tense body a little. "All right," I said cautiously.

We followed Amnun for a few hundred paces, turning left, then right, and stopping at a building that looked just like all the others. I led the animals to the back through a narrow alley and tied them to a post, then we entered the building, following Amnun through a back door.

We reached his living quarters on the second floor, where a woman and two children – a boy and a girl of about ten years, waited.

"My family," said Amnun, "Amina, my wife, and our twin children, Anat and Elazar. Please, sit down and rest yourselves from your journey."

Seeing his pleasant family helped make me feel a little safer. We sat, and I asked the question that had been bothering me for the several minutes since we met. "How did you know my name?"

He looked over at his wife and smiled, then back at me. "I knew you were coming. I was told, in a dream – by an angel! – that you would be arriving today – and I was shown your face, that I might know you. And I was commanded to take you in and help you, and your wife . . . and your *son.*"

The way he emphasized the last word – son – indicated he may know something of the importance of Jesus. I wanted to believe this man –

and all indications were that he was being truthful and trustworthy. But I wanted to be sure.

"This angel – did he tell you his name?"

"Gabriel."

With that one word, Mary and I both exhaled a sign of relief and smiled at each other.

"We know him," I said, now grinning. "Praise be to God."

"Gabriel!" Jesus repeated with a joyous smile. Almost as if he knew.

We all laughed.

With all the stress and fear surrounding our flight from Nazareth, and the hardships and concerns of our journey these past several days, it felt good to finally feel safe enough to enjoy some laughter.

And it felt good to have an ally here in this strange land of Egypt.

For the next few days, Amnun and his family allowed us to lodge with them, while Amnun and I went about in the day trying to obtain a place we could call our own – and also to establish some work for me.

With the wise men's gold coins, I did not have to work, but I did not feel right being idle. I had always worked – and Father had taught me it was important that a man always be engaged in something constructive – that it was good for his character. Besides, the gold – although abundant – was still limited, and there was no way of knowing how long we would be here, and if we may one day run out of that gifted resource.

I also did not want to draw undue attention to our family as a result of our temporary wealth. It may appear odd that we arrive in a humble caravan of donkeys only to be seen freely spending large quantities of gold without earning a living. Mary and I agreed it would be best to hold onto the gold as much as possible, only using it for emergency situations as needed.

We did, however, use it to obtain a place to live.

The home we rented consisted of two rooms on the ground floor of a limestone building not far from Amnun's home. The dwelling shared a kitchen with two other families. It was well-constructed, and allowed for privacy for our little family. We were able to keep our animals around back, near the shared water cistern.

We found the Shamar to be a vibrant, friendly district, with a synagogue only a few hundred paces from where we lived. Over the first few weeks, I spent many hours there, studying the scriptures intensely, hoping to find comfort and guidance – some sort of instruction to help me to know what to do in my role as husband to Mary in this strange land, and as father to Jesus.

I understood that I should be raising him to become a good man – to know the scriptures, and to choose rightly. I did my best to be a good example, and we studied the sacred texts together as a family. I considered that it was never too early to begin scripture reading with Jesus, since he seemed so intelligent and perceptive.

But two things caused me to struggle. First, Jesus seemed to need no correction from me – he never misbehaved. In fact, I found that he was the one teaching *me* so much every day. So, of course he would be a good man – with or without my influence. And second, if there was not much I could teach him in terms of normal upbringing, then there must be some other reason he was sent to Mary and I for his parenting. And that meant I needed to discover what it was that I, Joseph, had to offer him. What, I wondered, was *my* specific mission in raising the Messiah? What could I contribute?

So far, I had done all I was commanded – I married Mary, I knew her not until after Jesus was born, I kept Jesus safe and fed, and traveled here to Egypt to avoid danger as instructed. But what more – what else should I be doing?

Surely any man could do these very basic things. What was it that would distinguish me – how could I be *more* faithful? As a young man of barely twenty years old, I found myself lacking confidence. I could not help feeling inadequate, even though I was simply doing what was right. I was not reprimanded by God, and I was in fact very blessed – but I always felt that what I was doing for Jesus was never quite enough.

And so I studied, I fasted, and I prayed. And then studied, fasted and prayed some more.

I also talked with Mary.

One hot summer evening after I'd returned home from the synagogue, nearly a year after we'd arrived in the Shamar, after Jesus was asleep, I asked Mary, "Do you ever wonder – are we doing everything God wants us to do? Is there something more we should be doing?"

"For Jesus?"

"Yes, for Jesus."

She put her hand on my cheek. "Joseph, we have done exactly as we have been commanded. I do ponder all the things we've been through – in my heart I sometimes wonder what more is in store; and in my prayers, I ask for guidance – but I am assured we are doing exactly what we need to."

"Mary, I appreciate your comforting words. But – "

"Joseph. You are a good father."

I smiled a little, and kissed Mary on the cheek. "Thank you."

After a few minutes, Mary was asleep.

But I lay awake in the darkness, pondering. In the back of my mind, unformed questions swirled; deep in my heart, I felt incomplete somehow. I wanted to do more. I wanted to magnify my calling as the earthly father of Jesus – not merely be a good father.

Months passed, and we began to really get settled in our new life in the Shamar.

For the most part, we rarely ventured out into the rest of Alexandria. I occasionally did, for the purpose of working on a carpentry commission, but generally, our life revolved around our home and Amnun's home.

One winter afternoon we were all at Amnun's house, and several of Amnun's nieces and nephews were visiting from across the Shamar. Amnun and I sat watching the children play.

"Joseph," said Amnun, "have you ever noticed the way your son plays?"

"How do you mean?"

Amnun shook his head slowly, his gaze falling softly on Jesus. "He seems a natural leader, for one so young. Always a peacemaker, always kind. He shares freely, never cries out or causes trouble. Quite amazing, really."

"He has a wonderful mother," I said, smiling.

Amnun nodded. "Yes, Mary is a great woman, Joseph. But it seems there is something more. Something special." He leaned toward me and looked me in the eyes. "Joseph, we have not really spoken much about the day we met. It was a miraculous day, my friend. I have often wondered about the miracle – about the angel. I have not asked you about why you came here from Jerusalem – I have respected your private business. I only did as God told me. But I have asked God in prayer many times – I have asked why you were sent to us. I have not received a specific answer, but I have felt strongly that it has something to do with your truly wonderful son."

I stared at Amnun. I wasn't sure what to say. Mary and I had never shared our secret outside the family – and of course the shepherds and the wise men from the east – and Simeon and Anna at the temple. But surely I could trust Amnun. After all, Gabriel had appeared to him.

I closed my eyes for a few moments, and uttered a silent prayer, to confirm that it was right to share this sacred information with Amnun.

A moment later, my heart swelled.

It was right.

I took a deep breath and exhaled slowly. "Amnun, Jesus is the Son of God."

"Yes," said Amnun, "we are all sons of God."

"No, you do not understand, my friend. Jesus is the Messiah, the *very* Son of God."

Anmun looked confused for a moment, then stunned for a moment. Then a smile grew across his face, and he slowly nodded. "Yes. Yes, Joseph! Ha!" he clapped his hand on my knee. "It is as though I knew this all along, only . . . I did not know. But now it is confirmed. That is wonderful! Tell me about it – how it all came to pass. Tell me your whole story."

I spent the next hour or so describing everything to Amnun – from the first visit of Gabriel, to the most recent, when we were commanded to flee our home. Amnun sat in rapt silence, not even interrupting to ask questions.

Finally, as I finished the story with our arrival at the Shamar, Mary walked in with Amina. The woman had the same awestruck look on her face as her husband, Amnun. I looked at Mary, and her expression told me she had just finished telling Amina the same story I had just told Amnun. I smiled at Mary, and she returned the look. I'm sure we were both thinking it amusing that we'd chosen the same occasion to let our closest friends in on our secret.

Somehow, I felt like a burden had been lifted from my chest. In all my simple life, I had never been accustomed to keeping special private confidences and living in the shadow of a great secret.

From this moment on, our bond with Amnun

and his family was even closer. Over the following several months, we spent a great deal of time together – speaking not only of the mundane, daily aspects of life – but of the deeper, more meaningful things of God. And Amnun behaved more protectively of Jesus than he did of his own children, it seemed – a self-appointed guardian, to assist me in my role of protector of the family. And truthfully, I welcomed his attitude of service. It was not easy living in a strange land, always feeling – despite having settled in well at the Shamar – that I had to look over my shoulder at all times.

There were days that I was calm and free of the weariness, and other days that it seemed an assassin lurked around every corner of the Shamar. Sometimes it seemed the constant concern would make me grow old with worry.

And then, one night, as I laid down to another fitful sleep filled with dreams of Herod's men chasing Jesus through the streets of the Shamar, I received another visit from our trusty, majestic angel, Gabriel.

His brilliance and goodness immediately dispelled the dark dream, filling my bosom with peace.

"Hail, Joseph. I have a message from God."

"I am listening, and will go and do whatever the Lord requires," I said.

Gabriel smiled. "Yes, I know you will, Joseph. Arise, and take the young child and his mother, and go into the land of Israel. For those who sought the young child's life are now dead."

"Dead? Herod is dead?"

"Indeed. The child will be safe. Go now."

I awoke, feeling the same as I had the last time I'd had such a heavenly visit.

Heart strong, mind clear, senses sharp.

Limbs tingling.

Exhausted, yet somehow filled with energy.

I awoke Mary, and told her it was time for us to leave.

Time to return home.

CHAPTER IX – A HEARTBREAKING RETURN

Mary placed the last of our belongings in the pack on her donkey, then looked over at me. Her eyes were filled with tears.

"Although we have longed to be home," she said, "my feelings are so divided, now. I will miss our friends so much."

"Yes," I said, taking Jesus by the hand, "it is a difficult thing. I want to be home, yet part of me wishes to remain with these good people."

"It will be all right, Father," said Jesus, squeezing my hand. "You will see Amnun again."

I looked down at Jesus. What a profound thing to say, for a boy of barely four years old. And what peace filled my heart at his words.

"Thank you, Jesus," I said.

We walked back in to bid a final farewell to Amnun, Amina, and the children. They had come to help us with our departure.

I embraced Amnun. "My friend. Thank you for all you have done. We will never forget you and your beloved family. Be well."

"It has been a great honor," he said. "May God bless you and watch over you."

Mary and Amina exchanged their own goodbyes, and the children all hugged Jesus. We went back outside into the bright morning sun and mounted our animals, well-prepared for the long journey ahead.

We departed the Shamar, and headed east across the Nile Delta. Far to the south, we could see the ancient pyramids poking up above the distant horizon. It was strange to think that they were built by the slave labor of our forefathers, so long ago.

Somehow, our journey home felt much faster – and certainly less frightening – than our trek outward two years before. Several days after we set off from Alexandria, we were tired, but feeling good as we approached Hebron.

Evening was coming on, but we decided to push through to Jerusalem. We both longed to see the temple, and decided we could stay at the home of my father's uncle's friend – where we had stayed at the time Jesus was circumcised and presented at the temple.

"We could stay there for a few days, Mary. Attend the temple, replenish some supplies for the last leg of our journey. It will be a good chance to rest up in familiar surroundings once more."

"Yes," said Mary, "it is well."

We entered Hebron, and the streets were crowded with the usual evening bustle. As we continued through the streets, I began to feel strange inside. Something was not right, but I could not figure out what it was. Then I noticed people staring at us – in particular, staring at Jesus.

"Why are they staring?" I whispered to Mary.

"I do not know."

"You must not be from around here," said a morose-looking young woman with tired eyes that looked decades beyond her years. She spoke to Mary, but stared woefully at Jesus.

"No, we are passing through," Mary said. "Why?"

The woman squinted at Jesus through tears forming in her eyes. "There are no boys his age around here. Not anymore." She began to weep. "Not . . . anymore."

I frowned. "What – what do you mean, not anymore?"

Through her sobs, she said, "He killed them – he killed them all! All the little boys, Herod had them murdered. They say he was jealous of a new prophesied king, born at Bethlehem. So, he sent his soldiers – they slaughtered every last boy in the land round about Judea – including my son, Nathan. My husband was killed while trying to protect Nathan."

My heart ached. For this woman, and for all the families, for all the innocents who'd been killed.

I turned to Mary, and she was weeping – and holding Jesus close. Jesus was gently stroking her hair, looking sad.

"I am unable to say how terrible I feel for you," I said to the crying woman. "For all. We…we must keep going now."

We continued on, stunned at this heartbreaking news.

All the young boys . . . just killed? It was too

much to bear. What kind of evil could do such a thing? To slaughter innocent babies?

And yet, Jesus was saved from this destruction – we had been kept safe by fleeing to Egypt.

We continued to walk in silence, pondering what this meant.

Soon we could see the great city of Jerusalem. In the distance, a man walking with a pack animal came toward us from the direction of the city.

"Hail, traveler," said the man.

"Hail," I said.

"Are you going to Jerusalem?" he asked, staring at Jesus in a similar fashion as the woman in Hebron.

"Yes. We have come a great distance, after a long absence – about two years. We are on our way home."

The man shook his head. "Jerusalem. It is not the same as you remember it, I fear. There is great turmoil right now."

"Turmoil?" I asked, still recovering from the news of the children who'd been massacred, and suddenly fearing the worst. "What kind of turmoil?"

"You must not have heard, being gone so long. Just last week, thousands of angry men gathered on the temple mount. They were rebelling against Herod's son, Archelaus, who now rules. They were seeking relief from high taxes and a lack of employment. They also demanded freedom for political prisoners – and tried to appoint their own high priest to preside over the temple."

"What happened?" I asked.

He looked at the ground. "It was awful.

Archelaus sent squads of soldiers against our people. More than three thousand of our brethren were killed in the battle – more a massacre than a fight – including two of my brothers."

"Oh, I am sorry," I said. "This is very troubling. Is there still violence going on?"

"Not at this moment," he said. "But the peace is fragile. There is much suspicion and unease among the people. I fear the fighting could return any time. My father and mother buried my brothers, and told me to go away, that I would not end up like them. I am not a fighter, but I did believe in their cause. My father and mother are right – I should go away for a time, until things become settled."

"I see," I said. "I appreciate the warning. We will take caution as we travel."

"Farewell, traveler," he said, and carried on his way slowly, looking downtrodden.

"I am very concerned," I said to Mary. I looked up at the darkening sky. "Let us encamp here for the night. In the morning, we can decide how to proceed."

That night, Gabriel visited me once more.

"Joseph. You shall avoid Judea, stay away from Jerusalem for now. You will see the temple at a future time. Tomorrow, pass by the city on the west, and return to Nazareth without delay. Go home, Joseph."

The next morning, we complied.

With heavy hearts, we packed up and took the westward trail, skirting Jerusalem at a distance. As we traveled, I thought about the awful terror all those young families must have experienced as sword-wielding soldiers burst into their homes and brutally murdered their little boys. I imagined how many of them must have been running, their small boys in their arms, trying to escape the bloodshed, only to have their babies wrenched from their arms and hewn down by the sword. I wondered how many sacrificed their own lives in a futile attempt to save their children. My heart swelled with such sadness, tears streamed down my face. What great lamentation must have filled the land, what emptiness and sorrow.

In the face of such tragedy, how many had lost their faith, wondering if they had been abandoned by God?

Mary must have been pondering on the same subject, for she said, "Joseph, do you think my cousin Elizabeth – do you think they have also killed John?"

I breathed a heavy sigh. "I do not know – I can only believe that if he was prophesied to do great works among the people – to prepare the way for the Messiah – that he must have somehow been spared. For, as we know, the purposes of God are never frustrated by the evils of men."

She nodded, seemingly taking some small comfort in my words. "When we arrive home, perhaps my family will know."

We continued on in silence.

The land seemed filled with an oppressive feeling of death. It had been a long time since the slaughter of the innocents, but the wound was fresh to our sensibilities. I looked at Jesus, relieved that he had not been killed. Although I knew he had special protection, and a great mission to fulfill – and that it meant he would be spared until he was somehow raised up as king – I could not help but feel grateful we had been in Egypt and missed the horrors that had taken place here in our absence.

I understood that our son – God's son – would be kept safe, yet I often wondered where my efforts left off and God's wisdom began. Surely I had to keep him safe as any parent keeps their child from harm, yet part of me knew that if I made a mistake, God would make sure he would still be all right. However, as I considered that I had been the one entrusted with his care, I felt an extra obligation to go above and beyond – to be particularly cautious, to be better than any other parent.

And as he, at such a young age, continued to teach me great things – faith, patience, kindness – I wondered what I could possibly have to offer the Messiah, as his earthly father.

These concerns made my sleep restless – and it didn't help that as I laid down each night, a part of me wondered if I was going to receive another heavenly visit from Gabriel, giving me further instruction.

But Gabriel did not come.

We arrived back in Nazareth late at night – much as we had left, only not in so much of a hurry. It was an odd, breathtaking feeling of joy that struck my heart as I saw my father's house, and then our little home across the field behind it.

At last, after a hasty escape, long journey, and two years in exile; after the development of a close and wonderful friendship, another two visits from

an angel, and news of the horrors we had left
behind; we were home.

CHAPTER X – A SCARE, AND A REMINDER

John was gone.

He had not been killed in Herod's slaughter – he had been whisked away into the wilderness by his mother, Elizabeth. Zacharias had shared that information with Mary's father – but he had refused to share it with Herod's soldiers, so they killed him – right between the temple and the altar.

Mary and I both wept when we heard this. And Zacharias was not the only parent to die in the defense of a little son – it turned out many had fallen in this manner.

Elizabeth and John did not return – we assume they continued to live in the wilderness all these years – either fearful to return, or specifically instructed of God to remain there.

Meanwhile, time passed on for us as well, and our family grew, as sons and daughters came along, one by one.

First, James, who joined us within a year of our

return to Nazareth. Then Joses, Simon and Judas, in quick succession. And then the twin girls – Abish and Ruth; then Hannah; and finally little Benjamin.

As our family grew, so did our house – I added rooms to the back and to the east side to accommodate the children.

Mary and I made a decision to not share with our children the miraculous and wonderful reality of who Jesus really was. We felt that as children, they may not understand – and we did not want to create any contention that may arise if they thought that we considered Jesus to be more special than any of them. He was the eldest, so he still occupied a preeminent position among the children – that would be enough for now.

So, our family went on, as any other family. We decided the children would learn the truth for themselves – either through personal revelation, or along with the rest of the world, when the time was right – so our family life was normal, for the greater part.

We all loved each other dearly. All the children looked up to Jesus, and he taught them well – a perfect example.

Of course, not every day in our household was perfect. In fact, one time, I became so worried, I was near despair.

We had all traveled as a family – with my father's family in our company, including my siblings and their children – a large group of us, to Jerusalem. It was the Passover, and this was our annual trip for the Passover feast. Jesus had turned twelve years old just days earlier.

When the feast was over, and our visiting

complete, we took up our caravan and headed back toward Nazareth.

"It was a good feast, was it not?" asked my father as we finished up our first day's journey and began to set up camp.

"Yes," I said. "It is always good to visit the temple – and to see the people we know in Jerusalem."

"This was the most pleasant Passover trip in many years," added Mary. "I truly felt the Spirit at the temple."

"And of course," I said, smiling, "the feast of unleavened bread was wonderful."

"Joseph," said Father, "will you gather your boys to help with my tent? "

"Yes. James," I said, speaking to our second eldest boy, "go find Jesus and your other brothers."

I lifted my father's tent down from one of our animals and unpacked it on the ground. As the sun sunk lower in the sky, setting a deep orange hue on our encampment, I started to wonder if James had become distracted and forgotten his task to gather the boys. Then he came running up from behind me.

"Father," he panted, "I have looked everywhere – I have asked everyone in the company – nobody knows where Jesus is."

"What?" I said, standing up. "Surely he is here somewhere among our kinsfolk. Mary?"

"Yes," said Mary, who had been speaking with my mother.

"Jesus is missing."

Her face suddenly turned ashen, her eyes serious. "Have you spoken to all our kin?"

"James has. But let us do so again."

Mary and I split up, asking everyone in our large company about the last time they had seen Jesus. We came back together after our investigation.

"He is not here," I said.

"The last time anyone saw him was shortly before we left Jerusalem," said Mary.

I looked to the west and the sun was gone, only a quickly-diminishing glow remaining.

"I will go now," I said.

"I will come with you," Mary insisted, reaching out and grabbing my forearm as I turned to leave. "I will bring Benjamin as he is still nursing, but the rest of the children will be all right staying here with the family."

I nodded and checked the supplies on our best two donkeys. "Let us go."

We walked into the darkness as quickly as we could.

"Joseph, I feel that same anxiety – that same fear deep in my heart that makes me tremble – as I felt the night we fled our home to Egypt."

"I'm scared, too," I said. "I don't understand how this could have happened."

I then lapsed into silence, blaming myself and imagining the worst.

Yes, Jesus was the Messiah, and so he should be protected. But what if his mission was somehow dependent on his being taken care of properly and kept safe and raised up right? What if he was only *conditionally* the Messiah, and what if I had destroyed his future through my negligence? What if something awful had happened, and now another would be raised up to be the Messiah instead?

Had I failed my mission?

It had been so many years since my last angelic visitation, so many years since I'd received that direct guidance and comfort. And so many years since we'd really focused much on Jesus' prophesied future – our family settling into a state of normal development. Yes, Jesus was an extraordinary child, which was a subtle reminder to us of his true nature, but in our day to day life, we were not always thinking about his divine commission.

But now I was. And I was afraid I had jeopardized it somehow.

But coupled with that fear was a heavy grief. I was simply worried for my boy. Who was he with? What was happening to him? Was he hurt?

I loved Jesus. He was the Son of God, but he was also my son. The thought of him suffering in any way was almost too much to bear.

It seemed our feet could scarcely carry us fast enough as we returned to Jerusalem.

The journey back took all night. Having traveled all day the previous day, we were exhausted when we reached the city walls. But our concern for Jesus seemed to override our fatigue and push us onward as we frantically enquired after Jesus at every place we had been in Jerusalem over the past several days.

For three agonizing days and nights we searched, asked, cried. Jesus' disappearance broke our hearts, wore us out, dragged us down into the depths of despair.

We could barely sleep at night. We prayed without ceasing.

On the third day, I suggested we return once more to the temple. Although we had searched there without success, I felt that perhaps we could receive some inspiration there.

Anything.

As we entered, my heart leapt into my throat as I saw, sitting in the midst of the doctors and rabbis and wise old men, our beloved son! And, to our astonishment, he was calmly listening to them and asking them questions. The men who surrounded him were astonished at his answers to their questions – he was actually *teaching them.*

In this moment, as I saw him giving instruction to those who were supposed to have greater wisdom and learning and spiritual understanding – as I watched him profoundly educate and edify these leaders – it became clear who the real leader was. Who the real wise and wonderful One was.

It was so abundantly reinforced in me at that moment that my son – this astounding individual of only twelve years old – was indeed the very Son of God, the Messiah.

I swallowed hard and approached the group, my hands shaking from the emotional turmoil of having lost, and then found, Jesus.

Before I reached him, though, Mary had passed me by, rushing to embrace her son. With tears streaming down her face, she said in a tone not harsh, but full of concern, "Son, why have you dealt with us like this? Your father and I have sought you, sorrowing."

And Jesus said, "How is it that you sought me?

113

Don't you realize that I must be about my Father's business?"

At this point we were too overwhelmed from the harrowing experience to consider the full import of his words.

We were just glad to have him back, grateful that he was safe.

Jesus bade the men in the temple farewell, and they watched after us as we departed, murmuring in wonderment about how this young man could have such great understanding.

When we got outside the city walls, I began to calm myself once again, the relief settling over me like soft bedclothes. Recognizing that none of this was Jesus' fault – that he was still that perfect Son of God – that I had left him without realizing it – I fell to my knees in the dust and asked his forgiveness.

"Jesus, I am so sorry for leaving you behind – for not noticing you were not with us."

"I forgive you, Father," he said. "I was not afraid. When I did not know where you were, I simply went to the temple."

I stood, and we continued on our way. For the remainder of our return journey, Mary remained very quiet, clearly pondering all these events in her heart.

When we caught up to the rest of the family, everyone was relieved that we had been reunited, embracing Jesus warmly. As we continued our journey on the dusty road back to Nazareth, I wondered what Jesus had been teaching those men at the temple – and if he would teach those same things to me one day.

CHAPTER XI – DOUBTS & MIRACLES

Jesus continued to grow as any other young man – only he was always perfect, loving, kind, and thoughtful. He learned with speed and exactness, and taught his own family – Mary and I included – so much. He never sinned, and he always forgave quickly. He kept the peace in our home, and helped me focus on the eternal things – studying scriptures by my side, even helping me to understand them better. It was fascinating to me to see so much more than I ever had before in the scriptures – to see how everything pointed to him and his mission as Messiah.

As he became a man, he worked alongside me at my carpentry business, learning the trade from me as I had learned from my father.

The day arrived for Jesus' final lesson in carpentry – and I was reminded of my final lessons, which had occurred around the time that Mary and

115

I became betrothed. I showed Jesus the technique for the mortise and tenon joint, and he watched attentively, listening carefully. As I made the very last cut, I slipped and sliced the palm of my hand, near my thumb.

I winced and held it to stop the bleeding.

Jesus smiled.

I was surprised.

"Why are you smiling at my pain?" I asked, confused.

"I am not, Father. I am smiling because you have always been so patient, and I have never seen you become angry. Even now, as you have hurt yourself, you remain a great example."

I smiled back. "Thank you." His words humbled me.

That evening, I pondered his words, and wondered how he could consider me to be his example, when throughout his life he had always been showing me the way to be calm, kind, forgiving, obedient, and loving.

In fact, I had learned far more from Jesus, it seemed, than he had learned from me. Over the years, I had spent many times feeling so inadequate as a father – as the man bringing up the perfect son. I felt I could take no credit for anything good about Jesus.

As I ruminated on this subject, Mary came over and sat next to me.

"Well, Benjamin is asleep, at last. He seems to be feeling much better, though." Our youngest, now eight years old, had been ill the last few days. Mary noticed my somber expression and asked, "What's wrong, Joseph?"

I shook my head, then looked at Mary, still beautiful in the low light of the oil lamp. "Jesus. He is perfect, isn't he?"

"Yes, he has always been. What a blessing to us, to have him in our family. Of course, it makes it difficult to feel that we have much to contribute to his growth, doesn't it?"

She seemed, as always, to be reading my mind. "That is what troubles me. I often feel I should be doing something more – somehow being better than the best father on earth. After all, why else would God have chosen me to be his father? Yet, I also know that no matter what I do, I can never be enough – I can never add to his perfection."

Mary stroked my head. "I believe the answer is in the very words you just spoke. You were the one chosen to fill the vital and sacred role of raising Jesus. *You*. Not anyone else. You are the right man for the job, Joseph. And you are doing your very best. And that is all God could ask of us. I believe you are doing an admirable and wonderful job as father to Jesus – and father to our other children."

Her softly spoken words brought peace to my soul. "And you," I said, "are an ideal mother." I held her close. "And wife."

"How did it go today?" she asked.

"Very well, of course. Jesus is ready to begin his own carpentry shop – he has a great understanding of all aspects of the work. I just wonder…"

"Wonder at what point it's all going to change?"

"Yes. How long will life go on as normal, with Jesus working as a carpenter in our humble little city of Nazareth? Will he marry and have children here before – before whatever it is he will do as the

117

Messiah?"

"Well, I do not know at what point Jesus will begin his ministry as the Messiah, or when or how he will become king. But I do know this: he has always kept the law perfectly. That means he will continue to keep the law, and that means he will do all that is expected of him as a young man. You know what the elders always say."

"Yes – the Mishnah states that an unmarried man is always thinking of sin, and that he should marry by no later than twenty-four years old."

"I wonder what kind of woman would be the wife of the Messiah," Mary mused.

"Surely, a woman like you," I said, "Virtuous, honest, obedient – a chosen woman."

Mary smiled, and I fell silent for a few moments, pondering.

"You look troubled again," said Mary.

"I am concerned. I was speaking with Dovev last week."

"Is he a full member of the Sanhedrin, now?"

"Yes – he was accepted after the last Passover. And he tells me the Sanhedrin has been becoming more and more interested in power these last few years. It troubles him. But it troubles me even more. How do you think they will react when a young man from Nazareth comes along claiming to be king? Will this not threaten them?"

Mary sighed. "Men and their power struggles. Should they not be overjoyed at the arrival of the Messiah?"

"You would reasonably hope so. But from the way Dovev describes these men, they may not be so happy about it at all."

Mary was now the one to silently ponder. After a minute, she looked me in the eyes, "Joseph, whatever happens, whatever trials may come – we will need to make sure that Jesus' future family is taken care of."

I nodded. "Yes, of course. We will do whatever is necessary to protect them, when the time comes."

Only a year after that conversation, I had a dream.

One of *those* dreams.

"Joseph," said the gleaming angel, with his deep, calm voice.

"Gabriel?"

"Yes, Joseph. I have a message for you. In the matter of arranging a marriage for Jesus, you are to select a young virgin named Mary, who is the daughter of your childhood friend Chinan – whose family moved to Magdala many years ago. Also, you shall move your family to Jerusalem. This is the will of God."

"I understand," I said, swallowing hard. "Is there – is there anything else I should know? Anything I should . . . be doing?"

"You are a faithful man, Joseph. Be well."

I awoke from the vision feeling as I had following other such experiences – exhausted, yet exhilarated. I stirred Mary and told her everything.

The next day, we began to make preparations for our move to Jerusalem.

We did not do so in haste, as when we fled to

Egypt. Gabriel had not instructed us to tarry, but he had also not indicated any sense of urgency or danger. Thus, I spent the next several days wrapping up various carpentry business dealings and settling matters on our property. Since Gabriel did not say (as he had before) that he would be calling us back at a later time, we assumed this was to be a permanent move, and handled our affairs accordingly.

This included a tearful farewell to both my family and Mary's.

"May God go before you, and behind you, and bear you up in safety," said my father, as we departed. Leaning close to me with a hand on my shoulder, he whispered, "And do take care of your eldest – I know great things are ahead. Please send me word when his true identity is made known."

"Of course," I said. "We will see one another again very soon – there will be a betrothal in the near future."

Father nodded sagely. "Ah yes, of course. A queen for our future king, yes?"

"Yes," I said. "It would seem so. Farewell, Father."

I led our family – Mary, Jesus, and the other children, southward out of Nazareth. The morning was bright and cool, with a thin mist lying in patches around the base of the hills, mingling with the vineyards. The familiar and pleasant scent of olive trees mingled with some flowering sabras somehow brightened my mood and reminded me that we were doing as we had been commanded, and thus everything would be all right.

Our caravan consisted of several pack animals

on which we carried all of our belongings and provisions. The children all seemed to be in bright spirits also, as if this grand adventure could bring nothing but joy. The good feelings of our family helped make the journey seem to go by quickly, and we arrived at our destination without incident.

I was pleased to be greeted at Jerusalem by my old friend Dovev, who welcomed our family into his spacious home for the first few days while we got ourselves established. Although I had not seen him in nearly a year – since our last trip to Jerusalem for the Passover – it was as if no time had passed at all. That was the kind of friendship we had.

It was not long before I was able to obtain permanent lodgings for us in the northeast quarter of the city.

Our third day at our new home, I left the house to meet with a cousin of Dovev, who had told Dovev he could make arrangements for me to join with another man in a thriving carpentry business located south of the temple. As I left the house, I literally ran into a man as he was walking around the corner of the building.

"Oh, I apologize," I said, grasping the man's forearm to help steady him.

"Joseph?" he asked.

I stared at him for a long moment, then recognition dawned on me. "Chinan? What are you doing here?"

"I could ask you the same, my friend. Do you live in this building?"

"Yes, we just moved here from Nazareth. You?"

"I moved my family here from Magdala nearly a

year ago. I live two houses to the north of here."

My mind reeled. Could it be anything but divinely appointed that I would meet Chinan here this day? That we would move in so close to the man whose daughter was to be betrothed to Jesus?

"Surely," I said, "God's hand is in this. We must speak more – later. Can you stop by tonight?"

"Certainly, Joseph," Chinan grinned.

I walked on, stunned by this turn of events, and eventually found myself outside the temple, where I met Dovev.

"Joseph," he said with a warm smile and an extended hand. We embraced briefly, and he said, "come – I have much to talk to you about."

I followed him across the street and down a narrow passageway between the buildings, and into a structure that he said housed his office – a room from which he conducted affairs as a member of the Sanhedrin. Dovev offered me some water to drink and we sat together.

"Joseph," he said, "my friend Elad will be here soon to discuss the business opportunity I told you about. I recommend you seek to purchase a majority share."

"You mean, buy him out?"

"No, just offer to take on more than half of the expenses – and the profits. He will talk like he is doing well – and the business is indeed strong – but I know he is having difficulty with his taxes. He will be relieved that you will be bringing some much-needed money to the operation, and you will in turn have the advantage of control of the shop."

"I see," I said. "And he will be all right with this arrangement?"

"Yes, I am certain of it."

"You are a shrewd businessman, Dovev. Always thinking strategically – seeing both sides."

"Thank you, friend. Such insights have served me well in my position on the Sanhedrin."

"I am sure," I said. "Are they still as power-hungry as ever?"

"It is unwise to speak of them in such manner," Dovev said softly, looking down. Then he looked up at me with a smile and whispered, "But yes, they are."

"And you?"

He shrugged. "Who doesn't like a little power?" Then he looked serious. "Of course, Joseph, what matters most to me is serving my God. I have no real influence on the council – yet. But one day, perhaps, I will be able to help them see that a lust for power is not the best path."

I clapped him on the shoulder and stood up, strolling to the small portal that overlooked the alley. "Ah, it appears your friend is arriving."

A few moments later, there was a knock at the door.

"Elad!" said Dovev warmly. "Come, come. This is Joseph, who I was telling you about."

I shook Elad's hand. He had a firm grip – as to be expected from a man in our line of work. His thick black hair had some speckles of white around the temples, as did his long, bushy beard. His deep brown eyes appeared serious and honest. "I am pleased to meet you," I said.

"Peace," he said earnestly, with a slight bow of his head. "I am honored to meet such a good friend of Dovev."

We sat and spoke for nearly an hour – Elad detailing the state of his carpentry business, describing his current contracts, explaining the relationships with local merchants. He told me about the eight young men he had working for him. And he openly described his tax problem. I was impressed with his candor. He was indeed a decent man.

I told him I could help him with the money problems. I did not explain how, but I knew that with plenty of gold remaining from what the magi had presented Jesus, it would be easy for me to cover his debts. The relief on his face told me everything I needed to know, and when I offered to purchase six tenths of the business, he readily accepted. He understood that would give me control of the enterprise, but seemed reconciled to it as we agreed upon a price. Perhaps he saw that such an arrangement was preferable to losing everything. I promised to treat him as a partner, not an employee, and he expressed his gratitude as we parted ways for the day. Tomorrow, I would begin the work at my new carpentry business.

"Well," said Dovev, after Elad had departed, "I think that went very well."

"Yes," I said, "Elad is a good man. And you have given me good advice. I think I will keep you around."

We laughed. "Oh, I will always be around, my friend," Dovev said, "to the end."

Once I had secured lodgings and work, the next

order of business for our family was the betrothal of Jesus.

Gabriel had given me clear instructions, and God had even placed Chinan directly in my path upon our arrival at Jerusalem. All that had to be done now was to make the necessary arrangements with my old childhood friend. I wondered how I would introduce Chinan to the idea – should I tell him of my vision? Explain who Jesus really was? What would be prudent?

Although unsure how to proceed, I did not believe I should waste any time in fulfilling the commandments of God, so I went directly home from Dovev's office and spoke with Jesus.

"I had a dream," I said.

"I know," he responded, his voice as calm as ever. "I am to wed."

I started to wonder if I would ever get used to that. He did not do it all the time, but with matters of importance, it seemed he always knew exactly what was on my mind – yet he always let me come to him and bring up the subject, whatever it may be.

"Yes, Jesus. I saw Chinan today – the father of Mary whom you are to wed. I intend to see him this evening, and make arrangements to meet for the betrothal negotiations."

"I will come," said Jesus.

"Of course," I said. "That is customary."

"I mean, I will come to your first meeting with Chinan."

"Oh," I said, surprised. "Very well."

Jesus smiled. "Don't worry, Father. It will all work out to the good of all involved."

I had come to recognize that such words from Jesus were all the comfort I needed.

That evening, Jesus, Mary and I walked to the house of Chinan. Since all the other children were old enough to take care of themselves, we left them at home.

Chinan's home was not far from ours, and appeared to be constructed in a very similar fashion. He greeted us at the door with a cheerful countenance.

"Joseph! Please, come in, come in. And this must be your wife, and your son?"

"Yes," I said. "This is Mary. Do you remember her from your childhood? She is a daughter of Amram."

"Ah, yes," Chinan said slowly. "From the low hills on the west of Nazareth?"

Mary nodded and smiled. "Yes, that is right."

"And this is Jesus," I said, placing my hand on Jesus' shoulder. "Our son."

Chinan looked into Jesus' eyes and reached out a hand. Then his face changed. His smile faded and his mouth dropped open as his knees buckled. I stepped forward to support him as he seemed to fall limp.

I walked him inside and helped him into a chair. His wife, whose name I did not yet know, scurried in and put her arm around her husband's neck, saying, "Chinan, are you all right? What is wrong?"

"He just collapsed as he was greeting us," I said.

"You must be Joseph," she said, looking up at me briefly before fixing her attention back on Chinan, who had a stunned look on his face, and seemed unable to speak.

"Yes," I said. "And this is my wife Mary, and our son Jesus."

"I am Shula." She turned to Chinan and gently shook his shoulders. "Chinan, Chinan. What is wrong?"

Chinan's eyes, which seemed to be looking beyond the miles, gradually focused on his wife's face. A peaceful look came over him as he took a deep breath and he said, "Shula. Shula – it is he. The face that was shown to me in my dream."

It quickly occurred to me that I did not have to worry about how to approach the subject of a betrothal arrangement. That work had already been done for me. I wondered if it had been Gabriel, or some other angelic messenger.

Jesus stepped forward. "Yes, Chinan. It is I."

At moments like this, I marveled that despite all that I knew, I understood so little. I was simply grateful that I had sufficient faith to negate the need to fully understand.

Chinan grasped Jesus' hands in his, and slid to his knees on the floor. He looked up into Jesus' eyes. "I – I was starting to doubt myself – to wonder if the dream had been real."

"I have felt that way sometimes, too," I said to Chinan. "I have also experienced several dreams of an astounding nature – wherein I have received angelic messengers. It is no mere chance that we have arrived in Jerusalem recently and that I met you in the street. I have come tonight, as you probably already know, to make arrangements for a betrothal."

"Betrothal?" The woman's voice was soft and sweet as she entered the room to see this unusual scene. She saw Chinan on his knees before Jesus and said, "Father? Why are you – "

She broke off when Jesus turned to her, his eyes meeting hers. "Mary," he said.

She took a sharp breath. Without taking her eyes off Jesus, she asked, "Father, is this the man – the one from your dream that you told us about?"

Chinan nodded.

Jesus smiled gently.

Mary stepped to the side and supported herself against the door frame with one hand. Her long, straight black hair shone in the lamp light as her eyes glistened. "I knew you would come," she whispered. A single tear fell from her left eye.

It seemed there would be little negotiating necessary in this betrothal discussion. I clasped my Mary's hand in mine as I stood and observed this scene unfold.

"Joseph," Chinan said, rising to his feet, "I do not understand all things. But I know that I have witnessed a miracle. Your son – there is something special about him, I know not what. But it is indeed God's will that he marry my eldest daughter, Mary. This I know."

"She is a fine virgin," said Shula, "honorable and true in all things. She will make an excellent wife."

Jesus nodded. "I know."

"We are prepared to offer whatever price you feel is appropriate," I said, remembering our seemingly inexhaustible supply of riches provided by the magi. "Name the amount, and it is yours."

Chinan took a ragged breath, still emotionally overcome. "My friend, I am not concerned with such details now. I know you are a noble man and that you will compensate according to the tradition. Let us sup together now, and simply enjoy ourselves."

We all moved into another room, where a table was prepared.

Jesus and Mary sat opposite each other and spoke in low tones with soft smiles.

Chinan, Shula, Mary and I spoke of the many things that had happened since our early days in Nazareth. Chinan had met Shula in Magdala, where young Mary and their other three children were born. They'd moved to Jerusalem only a year before, after Chinan had felt impressed to move his leatherwork business to the city. Over the past several months, Chinan and Shula had been worried about finding a suitable husband for Mary, since they did not know that many people in Jerusalem. And only three nights before, Chinan had had his dream, which he had chosen to share with Shula and Mary.

Given that most of our families were to the north and east of Jerusalem, we decided to hold the wedding at a more convenient location, in Cana, where my wife's aunt had a nice home we knew we would be welcome to use for the celebration.

The date was set – four months away – and we returned to our home.

That night, I said to Mary, "Well, the matter of Jesus' marriage is taken care of – and it didn't even require me to do much of anything."

"Nothing except be faithful, obedient, and open to the promptings of the Spirit of God," Mary said. "Which is more than many good men can say they have done."

As always, Mary helped me to feel like I mattered – that I was more than just along for the journey. "Thank you," I said.

The following four months seemed to pass swiftly as the waters of a mighty river. While I remained busy with Elad bringing the carpentry shop back into good monetary standing and working on new business, Mary and the children worked to make our new house a home.

Jesus labored alongside me at the shop, but also spent much of his time studying the scriptures alone, memorizing whole passages and pondering their deep and hidden meanings, meditating at the temple, and helping at home. He also took some time to make trips to the Sea of Galilee, where he made friends with some of the fishermen along the shore. He seemed to very much like being down at the water's edge. And the men he met there were very decent people – foremost among them Peter, John, Andrew, Philip and Nathanael. Several times we had these friends into our home for a meal, and Jesus would teach us all afterward.

His friends seemed to intuitively know there was something very special about Jesus. Here was this man of only twenty years old unfolding the mysteries of God to these men who were several years his senior – as well as instructing me, his father. But it was more than that – his teaching was not only authoritative and edifying, but it was powerfully carried into our hearts by the Spirit of

God.

My friend Dovev, who came to several of these learning suppers, as I called them, said as much to me. "Joseph," he said to me one night, after all the other guests had left, and Jesus had retired to sleep, "your son – his teaching is wonderful. Did you bring him up in this knowledge?"

"It is not I," I said. "Jesus came to earth with all of this understanding and wisdom already inside of him, I believe."

Dovev slowly shook his head in awe. "You are very blessed to have such a son in your home. He is so full of love, peace, and light – it is difficult to explain. I wish my brethren in the Sanhedrin could get a taste of his goodness."

"Dovev, you are a good man, and it is good that the Sanhedrin is blessed with your membership. But from what you've told me of their political appetites and other such workings, I worry that what Jesus has to offer may not be so well-accepted in that setting."

"Sadly, friend, you are probably right," Dovev admitted. "They are very focused on the letter of the law, and on their own advancement. They are good men, of course, but perhaps not interested right now in some of the great truths of which your son speaks so plainly and yet eloquently."

"Thank you for your continued friendship," I said. "Peace to you and your family."

Dovev departed, and I spoke with Mary before going to sleep.

"Mary, the wedding is next week. Are the children ready for the journey to Cana?"

"Yes. While you and Elad remain here to work, I

will take the children and go with Elad's wife and children to prepare the feast. We will meet my father's family there at my aunt's home, and your father's family will come shortly after. Jesus will arrive with his friends the next day, and then we'll just await you and Elad. Please do not forget to secure the extra wine we will need – there will be many guests over several days of celebration."

"Yes, of course," I said, but my mind was beginning to wander as I contemplated Jesus' future and quickly became very sleepy. "Good night, Mary."

Elad and I set off for Cana late in the morning on the third day of the week. Everyone else was already there waiting for us, as we had planned. We simply had too much work at the shop to be able to leave any earlier.

The journey passed quickly as Elad and I discussed our thriving business, talked about the latest whisperings we'd heard about the local government, and shared stories of raising a family.

"Of course," Elad said, "raising your family is, I am sure, unlike anyone else's experience doing so."

"Why do you say that?"

"Ah, Joseph, I know that you know what I mean. The groom at this wedding we are on our way to attend – he is unlike any other man. Many have noticed. I believe great things are ahead for him."

I looked ahead to the horizon, where small ripples rose in the afternoon heat. "Yes, you are right, my friend. There's no denying it – Jesus is indeed special. More than special."

"Well," said Elad, "he does have a very good father."

We walked on in silence for a while. "Elad?"

"Yes?"

"Do you ever feel that you are not – not quite worthy of a challenge or a blessing that has been placed in your life?"

"A challenge or a blessing? An interesting question. Some would say that challenges *are* blessings. And often the reverse is true."

"Well, yes – but have you felt that way?"

"Unworthy? Or simply not up to the task?"

"Yes, that is what I mean. Do you struggle to feel capable?"

"I have had that feeling at various times. Everyone does. Why?"

I continued to look ahead at the dusty road. I shook my head. "Never mind."

As the sun dipped lower to the west, we arrived at Cana and found the house of Mary's aunt, where the celebration was set to take place. We stabled our animals and I found Mary very busily giving instructions to one of her younger sisters and two of Elad's daughters.

"…and please make sure the bread is warm when it is set at the table. Thank you. Well, go on then!"

The girls scurried away to tend to the tasks with which they had been charged, and I approached Mary. She smiled when she saw me.

"Joseph! How was the journey? Is all well at the shop?"

I hugged her and told her all was well.

"Did you secure the additional wine?" she asked.

"Wine? What wine?"

She gave me a look that told me I had clearly forgotten something important. I bit my bottom lip.

"The extra wine I asked you to make sure we would have available for the feast, since we will have many people here. That wine."

"Ah, *that* wine. Yes. I mean, no – I apologize, I forgot about it."

"Well," she said, "I suppose we will have to hope that that which we have will last through the whole celebration." She turned to move to her next task. "It will be a miracle if it does," she added with a sigh.

I felt bad that I had forgotten the one thing she had asked of me, but with all that was going on at the shop, it seemed hard to remember every little thing. "I'm sorry," I offered again, but Mary was already catching the attention of her aunt, presumably to ask her a question.

I decided to seek out Jesus and see how he was doing.

As I walked the grounds of this lovely home set into the hillside, I came across Jesus sitting quietly under an olive tree, staring serenely toward the house.

"Jesus," I said as I approached, "it is good to see you."

He smiled and stood to greet me. We embraced. "Father, I am glad you have arrived. All is well."

At once I was at peace. "Come," I said, "I believe the preparations are nearly ready."

As was the custom, this, the formal betrothal ceremony, was the event at which the great celebration was to take place. Next month, Jesus and Mary would have their marriage solemnized by a rabbi – Rabbi Chaim, son of the rabbi who had officiated at my own wedding to Mary, and the man who would oversee the ritual of this betrothal event.

Jesus made his final preparations by retiring to a private room inside the house for several minutes. I assumed he was praying; that was usually what he did when he required time alone. After Jesus emerged, the ceremony commenced as Chinan led his daughter Mary out of the house and into the garden plaza to the south.

As is typical for these betrothals, the ceremony was brief. Chinan introduced Rabbi Chaim, and the rabbi pronounced a heartfelt blessing on the couple. We all bowed our heads as he then spoke a thoughtful prayer, petitioning Almighty God for peace and love in the new household that was being formed. I pondered on the idea that a more peaceful and loving home could never be found than one in which Jesus was the head. Jesus and Mary then affirmed their commitment to the vows the rabbi had explained, after which Rabbi Chaim verified the assent of both Chinan and I.

The rabbi then placed Mary's hand in Jesus' and they turned to face the assembled guests.

As a cool breeze signaled the setting of the sun, the atmosphere of the garden plaza warmed up with the sound of soft music. The feast underway, I wandered off a little way to catch my breath and gather my thoughts in a quiet place near the border of the property. At the house, now a five minute walk to my east, I could hear the murmur of happy family members as they consumed roasted veal, figs, honeycomb, and grapes.

And drank wine.

I was reminded of the possible shortage due to my error. Lost in thought, I turned to watch the last of the sunset colors disappear into darkness as stars began to appear in the heavens. A few moments later, I felt a hand on my shoulder.

"Mary? You startled me," I said.

"Yes, it's me," she said, smiling. "Were you expecting someone else?"

I grinned at her words, remembering the day our marriage had been arranged. It still felt like only yesterday, though so much had happened since.

"It looks as though everything has worked out wonderfully," she said. "Jesus is now married. To a fine young virgin."

"I never doubted it would all work out," I said. I looked toward the house again, and watched one of the men carry an empty vessel inside before returning back outside with what was clearly a full one, judging by his struggle to carry it. "The only thing I doubt is the supply of wine."

Mary, who was clearly more at peace now than she was earlier, just shrugged contentedly and said, "That too will work out. Never worry."

Several days passed, and the celebration continued, with some additional guests arriving from Nazareth and Magdala, while others who had been in attendance from the beginning returned to their various homes in Cana, Jerusalem, and the surrounding region. Between our family and Chinan's extensive family, and a good number of friends, there was a constant coming and going of well-wishers – eating, drinking, talking, laughing and dancing.

Although the wedding was taking place at my wife's aunt's home, the matron of the house had placed Mary in charge of the festivities, since she was the mother of the groom. As hostess, it was Mary's responsibility to ensure the guests were well-fed and entertained – an exhausting task.

Near the end of the fifth day, Mary became aware that the wine supply was indeed not going to last. I watched as she spoke to her aunt's servants, and as each of them shook their heads in mute reply. Then I watched as she sought out Jesus. The servants followed her, and she found him seated at a small table near me, conversing with his friends Peter and John.

"Jesus," she said, "the wine is all gone."

Jesus turned to her and said in a low voice, "Mother, there is still more time – see the many guests who are not yet ready to leave. What would you have me do?"

Mary took his hand and simply said, "I do not know. But I know that you can do what is necessary." Then she said to the servants, "Whatever he says to you, just do it, all right?"

They nodded together.

Alongside the main doorway to the house, there were six stone water pots set there for cleansing –

probably enough to hold two or three firkins apiece. Jesus pointed toward them and said to the servants, "Fill the water pots with water."

And they immediately went and did as he said, filling them up to the very brim.

Then Jesus said to them, "Now draw out of the vessels, and bear the liquid to the governor of the feast – my mother's uncle."

And I watched as they did so.

When Mary's uncle tasted the water, he exclaimed, "Jesus! Ha ha! Such good wine you have brought forth! You know, it is common for every man, at the beginning of a feast such as this, to set forth the best wine; and then when all have consumed well for a few days, to bring out that which is worse. But you have kept the good wine until now! Saving the best for last...very nice!"

The servants all looked into the vessels with shocked expressions – one was even so bold as to dip a finger and take a taste. They then set about quickly to serving the new wine to other guests.

Mary turned to me. I knew what she was thinking: that it had indeed all worked out, as she had said it would. And I believe she knew what I was thinking: that this was only to be the beginning of the miracles.

Jesus' friends gathered round him and I heard them say that they were not only friends now, but they were indeed his disciples.

And I was once again struck with the powerful recognition that my son – the Son of God – was in our midst, and perhaps on the cusp of revealing himself to the world.

#

Following the official wedding one month later, Jesus and Mary established a home only a five minute walk from my carpentry shop in Jerusalem. As we got to know Mary better, it became clear that she knew exactly who she was married to – that Jesus was the Son of God. Whether he had told her directly, or if it had been made known to her by an angelic messenger, I did not know. But she clearly understood.

Two years after the wedding, a daughter, Malka, was born. Another four years, and along came a second daughter, Eliora.

As I watched Jesus with his wife, Mary, and with his little girls, I observed a man so full of love and patience, so kind and gentle, and so strong with the Spirit of God. He amazed me every time I saw him interact with his children. He was always teaching, always guiding with a soft but steady hand and piercing intellect. He taught them the scriptures with in-depth insights, and admonished them constantly in the ways of God. Those little girls were growing up to be wise and true.

I was greatly humbled by Jesus' example as a father and husband. I was truly learning from the Master – one who needed no learning from men such as I.

CHAPTER XII – HIS MINISTRY BEGINS

When Jesus was about thirty years old, we heard rumors that made our hearts leap for joy.

"Do you believe it could be him?" Mary asked me one evening, after having heard more reports of a man named John preaching in the wilderness of Judea.

"I do not know," I admitted, "but I have an odd feeling inside – a sense that it is perhaps your long lost cousin. They say he is baptizing many. Word is that his message is one of preparation for the coming of the Messiah. That fits with what we know."

Mary nodded, her face containing her excitement. "Yes, it does. He preached baptism for the remission of sins – which is what Jesus has been telling us about for years now. And this John, the Baptist, he is said to have grown up in the wilderness, feeding on locusts and honey. Perhaps all this time, he was kept safe by Elizabeth."

"Yes. Of course, Elizabeth was well-stricken in years when she bare John – it is unlikely she still lives at this day."

Mary bowed her head solemnly. "I know. I shall never see her again. But this word of John, if true, is still good news."

Jesus stepped in at that moment. "You shall see her again," he said reassuringly. "In the next life. And what you have heard of John – it is indeed the truth. He is the greatest prophet ever born – even greater than a prophet. I go to see him tomorrow. You should come."

It was an invitation we would not refuse.

The next day, Jesus, Mary and the girls, along with Mary and I and our two youngest children, made our way out of Jerusalem, navigating the busy streets until we reached the city wall. There, we came across my friend Dovev.

"Hail, Dovev!" I said. "What brings you here?"

"I was running a message for some higher-ranking members of the Sanhedrin," he said by way of explanation. "But I am done with that task now. Where are you headed?"

"We are going to the River Jordan – to see John the Baptist. Do you wish to join us?"

"Certainly, thank you."

Our little group continued on, and soon we found ourselves approaching a crowd of about fifty people. Standing in their midst was a tall man, whose clothing consisted of nothing more than a loose-fitting garment of camel's hair and a leather girdle to cover his loins. His hair was dark and full, along with his long, bushy beard. His dark eyes seemed to shine with intensity as he spoke.

Preaching loudly, he said, "Repent, for the kingdom of heaven is at hand! Soon, one will come who is far mightier than I am. In fact, I am not even worthy to stoop down and unloose the latchet of his shoes. Yes, I have baptized many of you with water, but he will baptize you with the Holy Ghost!"

When he saw Dovev – clearly a member of the Sanhedrin because of his robes – approaching, he turned and said, "Oh, you generation of vipers, who warned you to flee from the wrath to come? If you are serious, you must bring forth fruits that show you are truly repentant and ready for this ordinance. You cannot just think within yourself, 'I am a son of Abraham, and that is enough.' Heh. God could take these stones here at my feet and raise up children unto Abraham. No, no, the blood of your lineage is not enough to save you. Are you ready, in your heart, for the baptism of the Holy Ghost?"

Dovev was taken aback by these words directed right at him. From his face, it seemed he thought the words harsh – but my father always said that the wicked take the truth to be hard. Not that Dovev was a wicked man, but John had made it clear that the path of the Pharisees was one of hypocrisy.

For his part, Dovev, who had merely come along to observe, said as much. "I have come to see what you preach, Baptist. I have come with my friends to learn – not to cause you trouble. Continue with your preaching and baptizing, if you desire."

Then Jesus stepped out from behind Dovev, and somehow John recognized him. He fell to his knees as Jesus walked forward to greet him.

"It is you," John whispered.

Jesus smiled. "Cousin, will you baptize me?"

But John shook his head. "Jesus, I need to be baptized of you, and yet – you come to *me?"*

"Suffer me to be baptized of you, for it needs to be done in order for me to fulfill all righteousness. It is a commandment of my Father – and so I will keep it."

John, tears flowing from his eyes, nodded.

The two men went down into the water, and John baptized Jesus, immersing him fully in the slow-moving waters of the river.

And then the most amazing thing took place.

As Jesus came up out of the water, John looked up. At first, I could see nothing, but then it seemed as though the heavens opened – and I saw a bright white light that looked like a dove descend and land upon Jesus.

And then there was the Voice.

It seemed to come from heaven. It said, in a rich, warm voice that penetrated to my very soul, "This is my beloved Son, in whom I am well pleased. Hear him."

And then Jesus spoke to us. He quoted scriptures – Isaiah, Jeremiah, Malachi. He said that his time had now come – that he had a work to do. He also admonished us to follow his example – so everyone in our group – except Dovev – went down into the water and was baptized of John.

The water was cool, but my heart was warm.

My spirit seemed to be soaring atop the clouds

as we made our journey home.

I looked at Mary as we reached the walls of Jerusalem.

"It has begun," I said.

It was not long after that the Passover was at hand, and we all gathered for the feast days.

When we went to the temple as a family on the third day, the holy place was filled with those who sold oxen and sheep and doves; and those who changed money, sitting and conducting their business.

We entered the temple, our hearts full. But Jesus' face fell from a smile to a stern frown. Before I could say anything, he set about to make himself a whip out of small cords.

And then he went to work.

With swift justice, he drove all of the merchants from the temple. He drove out their sheep, and their oxen – and he even poured out the changers' money. And in a final act of righteous indignation, he overturned their tables.

The cages and bowls and money crashed to the floor and scattered – much like the surprised vendors.

Finally, Jesus spoke. To those who sold doves, he declared, "Take these things out of here! Do not make my Father's house a house of merchandise!"

I was quite taken aback.

I had never seen Jesus so animated, so full of passion and fire. Clearly, he reverenced the temple, and could not bear to see it defiled.

I grasped Mary's hand, smiled, and stood there as a proud father.

Two weeks later, Mary, Jesus' wife, came to see Mary and me.

"You seem concerned," my wife said, noticing the heavy look in Mary's eyes.

"It is well," Mary said. "I am just tired. The girls have been fevered for a few days, but are better now. Jesus blessed them, and they immediately got better. I am now catching up on my rest."

"There's something more," I prompted.

"It's Jesus. Last night, he told me he was going to the desert to fast and pray. He told me he would be gone for some time – it is in preparation for commencing his work."

"Yes," I said slowly, "his mission is starting now. He had told me something of this a while back. He is intending to fast for forty days."

"Would you like to bring the girls here – stay with us during this time?" my wife immediately offered.

Mary exhaled. She seemed suddenly relieved. "Could we? That would really help."

"Of course," I said. "We'd love to have you and our grandchildren here with us."

And so Mary and the girls moved in with us.

I know it had to be hard for them – not living with us, but worrying about Jesus. As his father, I certainly struggled deeply during this time. Forty days is a long time to be away, and an unheard-of period for a fast. I found myself torn between the natural worry of a parent who loves his son, and the faith I knew I should have.

Of course, I told myself, Jesus can take care of himself. Of course he will be all right. He knows what he is doing. He is the Messiah – he will not come to harm. He is just readying himself for what is ahead.

But what, I wondered, really was ahead?

Despite the reassurances I tried to give myself, there were still some days that I could barely stop myself from going out and searching for him – but I knew I must not interfere in this. It was his preparation time. I had to simply resist the urge to find Jesus and seek for peace instead.

Finally, those long forty days and nights had passed, and Jesus returned from the wilderness. He looked leaner, yet stronger. As a carpenter, he had grown strong muscles over the years; now, much of that had melted away to reveal a very slender man. Although his face was slim and his eyes a little sunken, they sparkled with power like never before. He seemed to have a new resolve about him, and a sharp alertness as if all his senses had been heightened by his experience – yet he also exuded calm, serenity, and warmth. He had always seemed sure and steady, and it was hard to imagine him being even more stalwart – yet somehow he now was.

That night, he recounted an important part of his experience to our whole family.

"Toward the end, after I had spent much time communing with the Father, as I was at my weakest, physically – very hungry and weary – the Adversary came to me to tempt me. He told me, 'If you are really the Son of God, command that these stones be turned into bread.' But I answered and said, 'It is written, man shall not live by bread alone, but by every word that proceeds from the mouth of God. Revelation is the greatest sustenance of all – of far greater eternal value than food for the body."

I considered how Jesus had once turned water into wine, and, knowing he had the power, I was astounded by the kind of strength it must have required to resist the temptation to simply turn those stones into bread and feed his morbidly empty belly.

Jesus continued. "Then I was taken up and the Spirit set me on a pinnacle of the temple, and the Adversary came and said to me, 'If you really are the Son of God, cast yourself down. For it is written, he shall give his angels charge concerning you, and in their hands they shall bear you up, lest at any time you dash your foot against a stone."

"What happened?" asked Benjamin.

"I simply said to him, 'It is written again, you shall not tempt the Lord God.' Evil will try to look good – even by quoting scripture – but it is all counterfeit. Benjamin, my dear little brother, it is imperative to know, understand, and *apply* the scriptures."

Indeed. Jesus had the power to do anything – but he had no need to prove himself to the devil.

"And again," said Jesus, "I was in the Spirit, and I was taken up to an exceedingly high mountain, and I could see all the kingdoms of the world, and the glory of them. And the Deceiver came once more and said, 'I will give you all these things if you will just fall down and worship me.' This was a foolish and vain attempt. He surely knows I will inherit all that my Father has. Perhaps he thought I would be tempted by the ease of the way. But he simply could not understand – will never understand – that I love my Father, and would rather serve him with no reward than worship a fallen angel and receive all. So I said to him, 'Leave me, Satan, for it is written, 'You shall worship the Lord God, and him only shall you serve.' He may no longer comprehend love, but he still knows what obedience means – even if he has abandoned the principle."

"And then what happened, Father?" asked young Eliora.

Jesus completed his story. "Then the devil left me, as I had commanded him. And then I was ministered to by angels, who comforted me and strengthened me. And then I returned home."

"So," asked Mary his wife, "does this mean that you are ready?"

"Yes," Jesus answered. "The time has come."

The time had come indeed.

Jesus began to preach regularly – anywhere and everywhere people would listen. Within only a few days, he had many people following him from place to place to hear his powerful teachings.

To my surprise, he began to create an organization. He called apostles to learn of him and accompany him on his journeys, and to help teach his message. Of course, the first ones he called were his friends the fishermen – men who were already well acquainted with his profound instruction and who counted themselves believers. They were willing to readily abandon their business as fishermen and follow Jesus.

Mary and the children stayed with us from that time forth, as Jesus was now on a full-time mission – his destiny unfolding according to the words of Gabriel all those years ago.

After the first week of his ministering, Peter came by to visit and tell us about what was happening along their way. Jesus, he said, was still out teaching at that hour.

"And we went into Capernaum," he said, his voice and face animated with excitement. "And on the Sabbath day Jesus entered into the synagogue, and taught. John and Andrew were there, too. And everyone at the synagogue was astonished at the doctrine Jesus taught – for he taught them with power and authority, not like the scribes."

"Just as we have heard him teach," Mary said.

"Yes," I added, "even since he was only twelve years old and teaching in the temple."

Peter nodded and continued. "And in this synagogue there was a man with an unclean spirit. And he cried out, saying, 'Let us alone; what have we to do with you, Jesus of Nazareth? Have you come to destroy us? I know who you are – you are the Holy One of God.' And Jesus rebuked him – rebuked the evil spirit – saying, 'Hold your peace, and come out of him.' And the unclean spirit seemed to try to put up a fight, making the possessed man cry out, but then it came out of him! And we were all amazed! I heard people murmuring and wondering how Jesus had such authority to even command the unclean spirits."

I marveled at the story, yet part of me was not so surprised that Jesus was so powerful and authoritative.

"So," Peter finished, "I found that the story of what Jesus did has spread so fast, it arrived back here in Jerusalem before even I did! Everyone in Galilee is talking about it. I'm even hearing stories that he has done the same thing in other synagogues, casting out devils wherever he goes."

"Are you going back – to stay with him?" asked Mary.

"Oh yes," said Peter, "I will be meeting with Jesus and the other apostles tomorrow."

By the next week, the fame of Jesus was all about. I heard that he even healed a leper. Peter later told me that Jesus had asked the healed man to keep it quiet, but the man went out anyway and began to tell everybody, such that Jesus could not even openly enter into the city anymore, but spent his time in deserted places just so he could sleep and have a few moments for his private prayers. People who wanted to be healed and taught flocked to him from every quarter of the land.

One day, I took leave from the carpentry shop early and met Dovev. We wanted to visit with Jesus together – to see how he was doing.

"You know," he said to me as we walked the city streets, "I am not only going with you today out of personal interest. The Sanhedrin has asked me to report to them what I see and hear. They are concerned about the growing following of your son. They have spoken critically of him. While I do not agree with them that he is doing any harm, I am bound to tell them everything I observe."

"That should not be a problem," I said, "since we both know Jesus is not doing anything wrong."

Dovev nodded. "I know that. But you never know how my peers will choose to interpret the facts."

Jesus was easy to find – we merely followed the crowd.

We saw them heading for a large hill. Apparently, Jesus realized the only way he could teach such a multitude was to go up into a mountain. And there he went, with his apostles as well, to preach. Dovev and I found a place to sit and listen.

Jesus started speaking – and his words shot like arrows into my heart, penetrating to my center.

"Blessed are the poor in spirit who come unto me, for theirs is the kingdom of heaven. Blessed are those who mourn, for they will be comforted. Blessed are the meek, for they will inherit the earth. Blessed are those who hunger and thirst after righteousness, for they will be filled with the Holy Ghost. Blessed are the merciful, for they will obtain mercy. Blessed are the pure in heart, for they will see God. Blessed are the peacemakers, for they will be called the children of God. Blessed are those who are persecuted for righteousness' sake: for theirs is the kingdom of heaven. And blessed are you, when men revile you, and persecute you, and say all manner of evil against you falsely, for my sake."

I looked over at Dovev, and he was rapt. The rest of the crowd, too, sat in silent awe as these words touched their hearts.

"Rejoice, and be exceeding glad," Jesus continued, "for great is your reward in heaven. For they also persecuted the prophets who came before you. You are the salt of the earth: but if the salt has lost its savor, it is no longer of any use but to be cast out, and trodden under foot of men. You are the light of the world. A city that is set on a hill cannot be hid – neither do men light a candle, and put it under a bushel, but on a candlestick; and it gives light to all that are in the house. Let your light so shine before men, that they may see your good works, and glorify your Father in Heaven."

The breeze brushed my face, but my heart stayed warm as Jesus spoke.

"Don't think that I have come to destroy the law, or the prophets. I have not come to destroy, but to *fulfill*. For I say to you with great certainty and truth, until heaven and earth pass, not one jot or one tittle will pass from the law, until all is fulfilled. Whoever, therefore, breaks one of these least commandments, and teaches men to do so, he will be called the least in the kingdom of heaven; but whoever does and teaches them, the same will be called great in the kingdom of heaven. For I say to you that unless your righteousness exceeds the righteousness of the scribes and Pharisees, you will in no case enter into the kingdom of heaven."

At this remark, I looked to Dovev. He seemed to not be bothered by Jesus' pointed statement.

At this point, Jesus began to speak in a new direction. He appeared to be reinterpreting the Mosaic Law. Everyone seemed genuinely fascinated by this higher law he described.

"You have heard that it was said by those in days past, 'you shall not kill,' and whoever kills will be in danger of the judgment. But I say unto you that whoever is angry with his brother without a cause will be in danger of the judgment, and whoever derides his brother will be in danger of the council, and whoever calls his brother a fool will be in danger of hell fire. So do not come to the altar to offer up your sacrifices when you still have malice in your heart for your brother. Leave the sacrifice there, and go be reconciled to your brother, and then offer your sacrifice. Settle your arguments with your enemies quickly, so your contentions do not rage out of control. You have heard that it was said by those in days past, 'you shall not commit adultery.' But I say to you that whoever looks on a woman to lust after her has committed adultery with her already in his heart. And if your right eye offends you, pluck it out, and cast it away, for it is better that you lose a body part than to lose your soul."

Dovev turned to me and whispered, "Such fascinating doctrine. It is unlike what we have been teaching. But not entirely different. Just...better."

"It is the extension of all we have learned," I said. "It is what Jesus has been expressing through his words and actions for as long as I can remember. Now he is codifying it."

"...has been said by those in days past, 'you shall not forswear yourself, but shall perform unto the Lord your oaths.' But I say to you, do not swear at all; not by heaven; for it is God's throne – nor by the earth, for it is his footstool; not by Jerusalem, for it is the city of the great King. And do not swear by your head, because you cannot make even one hair white or black."

A few people smiled at that.

"But let your communication be, 'yes, yes; no, no,' anything more than that is evil. You have heard that it has been said, 'an eye for an eye, and a tooth for a tooth.' But I say to you, do not contend with evil – if someone strikes you on your right cheek, turn the other cheek to him also."

One man with a perpetually angry face shifted uncomfortably.

"And if any man will sue you at the law, and take away your coat, let him have your cloak also. And whoever compels you to go a mile, go with him two."

The squirming man got up and shuffled down the hill, glancing back darkly over his shoulder one time. I felt sorry for him.

"Give to he who asks of you, and from he who would borrow from you, don't turn him away. You have heard that it has been said, 'you shall love your neighbor, and hate your enemy.' But I say to you, *love* your enemies, bless those who curse you, do good to those who hate you, and pray for those who despitefully use you, and persecute you. Do this, so that you may be the children of your Father in Heaven – for he makes his sun rise on the evil and on the good, and sends rain on the just and on the unjust. For, if you love those who love you, what reward do you have? Do not even the publicans do the same? And if you salute your brethren only, how is that better than others? Do not even the publicans do so? Therefore, be perfect, even as your Father in Heaven is perfect."

Dovev turned to me. "Perfect? Perfect as God? That is a very difficult expectation, is it not, Joseph?"

I nodded. "Indeed it is. But you must remember, my friend, that which Isaiah prophesied. That we would have help in achieving that perfection. For we cannot do it alone."

Dovev nodded. "Yes. The promised Messiah. You know, Joseph – with the miracles that Jesus has been performing – well, I have heard some say that he is, himself, the Messiah."

I nodded, not fully realizing what Dovev had said, and directed his attention back to what Jesus was now saying.

"Take heed to not be visibly charitable, to be seen by men – otherwise you have no reward of your Father in Heaven. Therefore, when you do your alms, do not sound a trumpet before you, as the hypocrites do in the synagogues and in the streets, that they may have glory of men." A low murmur rolled through the crowd. "I say to you with certainty: they have their reward. But when you do your alms, do not let your left hand know what your right hand is doing. Your alms should be in secret – and your Father who sees in secret himself will reward you openly."

Dovev turned to me. "I like what he is saying, friend. I am concerned, though, that the Sanhedrin will not look favorably upon my report."

"He only speaks the truth," I said. "If you do the same, you should have nothing to fear."

"I fear for him, not myself," Dovev said. "The Sanhedrin is very powerful."

"...and when you pray," Jesus continued, "do

not be as the hypocrites – for they love to pray standing in the synagogues and in the corners of the streets, that they may be seen by their fellow men. I say to you with certainty, they have their reward. But you, when you pray, go into your closet, and when you have shut your door, pray to your Father who is in secret, and your Father who sees in secret will reward you openly. And when you pray, do not use vain repetitions, as the heathen do – for they think they will be heard because of their much speaking. Do not be like them – for your Father knows what things you have need of, before you even ask him."

I noted that one of Jesus' apostles was writing his words – and I was glad of it. Especially when Jesus uttered his next words – a lesson on prayer that I knew in my heart would be had for generations to come.

"You should pray in this manner: Our Father in Heaven, may your name be sanctified. Your kingdom comes; your will is done on earth, as it is in heaven. Today, provide us our daily bread. And forgive us our debts, as we forgive our debtors. And suffer us not to be led into temptation, but protect us from the evil one. For the kingdom and the power, and the glory are yours, forever. Amen."

"Amen," I whispered, and could hear others around me do the same.

Jesus continued his sermon. "For if you forgive men their trespasses, your Heavenly Father will also forgive you. But if you do not forgive men their trespasses, neither will your Father forgive your trespasses. Moreover, when you fast, do not be like the hypocrites, of a sad countenance – for they disfigure their faces so that they look like they are fasting. I say to you with certainty, they receive their reward. But you, when you fast, anoint your head, and wash your face, so that you do not appear to be fasting, and your Father who sees in secret will reward you openly."

"I am sensing a strong theme, here," said Dovev. "It is not about the outward appearance, but what is in the heart that matters in the eyes of God."

I considered my friend – how he appeared on the outside to be just another member of the Sanhedrin, but knowing that on the inside, in his heart, he was pure and good. Applying Jesus' sermon, this gave me great hope for him.

"And do not lay up treasures for yourselves on earth, where moths and rust can decay and destroy, and where thieves break through and steal – but lay up your treasures in heaven, where neither moth nor rust corrupt, and where thieves do not break through or steal. For where your treasure is, there will your heart be also." Jesus shifted his seating position to get more comfortable, as he got deeper into his explanation. "The light of the body is the eye. So if your eye is sincerely seeking the glory of God, your whole body will be full of light. But if your eye is evil, your whole body will be full of darkness. If, therefore, the light that is in you is really darkness, how great is that darkness! For no man can serve two masters – either he will hate the one, and love the other; or else he will hold to the one, and despise the other. You cannot serve God and the world."

I turned to Dovev. "You see, my friend, how he

is drawing stark lines."

Dovev looked at me. "Yes, Joseph. I see. This is what Gamaliel, and Nicodemus, and even Joseph of Arimethea have been saying when Jesus' strongest detractors in the Sanhedrin are not around. Gamaliel's liberal Hillel doctrines do not go over well among some of the Pharisees – but they have been influencing me." He said no more, but returned his attention to Jesus.

"Therefore I say to you, take no thought for your life, what you will eat, or what you will drink; nor for your body, what you will put on. Is not life more than meat, and the body more than clothing? Observe the fowls of the air: they do not sow, nor do they reap, nor gather into barns; yet your Heavenly Father feeds them. Are you not much better than them? Which of you, by taking thought, can add one cubit to his stature?"

Some in the audience looked around at one another, as if someone might actually speak up. Of course, however, no one did. Jesus' point was well made.

"...and why do you take thought for clothing? Consider the lilies of the field, how they grow; they do not toil, nor do they spin – and yet I say to you that even Solomon in all his glory was not arrayed like one of these. Wherefore, if God so clothes the grass of the field, which today is, and tomorrow is cast into the oven – shall he not much more clothe you, oh you of little faith?"

Suddenly, my concerns over our growing business, and providing for my family (and now Jesus' family), seemed to melt away like a morning dew. Yes, I had to do my part, but if I had faith, it would all work out and God would provide. Such a comforting thought!

"...therefore take no thought, saying, 'what shall we eat?' or, 'what shall we drink?' or, 'how shall we be clothed? Your Heavenly Father knows that you have need of all these things."

He paused and looked around at all – engaging, it seemed, each person with his eyes before speaking again. "But you should first seek the kingdom of God, and his righteousness – and all these things shall be added to you. Therefore, take no thought for tomorrow – it will take care of itself. Tomorrow has troubles of its own, without needing you to bring them into today."

He smiled, and it seemed like a sense of relief washed over the multitude.

"Do not judge unrighteously, or you will bring such judgment on yourself – but instead, judge righteous judgment. For you will be judged with the same judgment with which you judge, and as you measure out to others, it will be measured out to you. And why do you see the speck in your brother's eye, but do not even consider the beam that is in your own eye? Or how will you say to your brother, 'let me pull out the speck from your eye,' while a beam is in your own eye? You hypocrite – first cast out the beam from your own eye; and then will you see clearly to be able to remove the speck from your brother's eye."

The apostle who was writing Jesus' words quickly moved his scroll to a new section and continued to record the sermon.

"Go out into the world, saying to all, 'repent, for the kingdom of heaven has come.' And you should keep the mysteries of the kingdom to yourselves, for it is not wise to give that which is holy to the dogs, or to cast your pearls to swine, or they will trample them under their feet, and return to tear you up. For the world cannot receive that which you, yourselves, are not able to bear – so do not give your pearls to them. Ask, and it will be given to you; seek, and you will find; knock, and it will be opened to you. For everyone who asks receives; and he who seeks finds; and to he who knocks it will be opened."

"That is a wonderful promise," Dovev whispered.

"Yes," I said. "Jesus once explained to me that as long as you have aligned your will with the will of God, your prayers will be answered according to your desires."

Jesus seemed to be conferring with his apostles for a moment, then continued.

"Or what man is there of you whom if his son asks for bread, will he give him a stone? Or if he asks for a fish, will he give him a serpent? If you then, although wicked, know how to give good gifts to your children, how much more will your Father in Heaven give good things to those who ask him?"

Jesus raised his eyes to gaze out at the setting sun as it cast shadows across the hills.

"Therefore, all things that you want men to do to you, do the same to them – for this is the law and the prophets. Enter in at the strait gate, for wide is the gate and broad is the way that leads to destruction, and there are many who follow that way. Because strait is the gate and narrow is the way that leads to life, and there are few who find it."

The sun now behind the western hills, a cool breeze picked up and gave me a chill.

"Beware of false prophets," Jesus added, "that come to you in sheep's clothing, but inwardly are ravenous wolves. You will know them by their fruits. Do men gather grapes from thorns, or figs from thistles? Every good tree brings forth good fruit – but a corrupt tree brings forth evil fruit. A good tree cannot bring forth evil fruit, nor can a corrupt tree bring forth good fruit. Every tree that does not bring forth good fruit is cut down, and thrown into the fire. So, you will know them by their fruits."

"Interesting," said Dovev. "He explains first that it is what is on the inside that counts – the intentions of our hearts. But he does not stop there. It is also imperative that we actually do good works outwardly."

"Not everyone who says to me, 'Lord, Lord' will enter into the kingdom of heaven, only he who does the will of my Father in Heaven. Many will say to me in that day, 'Lord, Lord, have we not prophesied in your name? And in your name have cast out devils? And in your name done many wonderful works?' And then will I profess to them, 'I never knew you. Depart from me, you who work iniquity.' Therefore, whoever hears these sayings of mine, and does them, I will liken him to a wise man, who built his house on a rock. And the rain descended, and the floods came, and the winds blew, and beat upon that house; and it did not fall, for it was founded on a rock. And every one who hears these sayings of mine, and does not do them, is like a foolish man, who built his house on the sand. And the rain descended, and the floods came, and the winds blew, and beat on that house; and it fell – and great was the fall of it."

With that, he stopped speaking, and the multitude pondered quietly. Many seemed astonished at Jesus' teachings. Dovev was lost in thought. After a few minutes, several people got up and returned to their homes, but others remained.

Jesus then stood with his apostles and they made their way down the hillside.

"Come," I told Dovev, interrupting his pondering, "let us return home."

"No, it is all right," Dovev said, waving me off, "you go. I'd like to remain here for a while."

I nodded and went home to my Mary and the family.

"What news of Jesus," she asked, as soon as I arrived.

"He has offered a very powerful sermon," I said, "to a multitude, over on the mount. He is expounding much of the doctrines he has taught us – and more. I shall share it all with you tonight. Dovev was very touched. He stayed behind."

"Does he look well? Fed, rested?" asked Jesus' wife Mary.

"Dovev is healthy as ever," I said.

"No, Father, I meant Jesus. Is he well?"

"Yes," I said, smiling. "I knew what you meant. Your husband appears strong, healthy, full of the Spirit."

A few minutes later, someone knocked loudly at the door. I opened it to see Dovev, and he was out of breath.

"I ran . . . all the way . . . back," he panted. "Joseph . . . after everyone departed, and Jesus thought he was alone with his apostles – I watched as a leper came and bowed down before Jesus, and he said, 'Lord, if you will, you can make me clean.' And Jesus put out his hand, and touched him, saying, 'I will; be clean.' And immediately his leprosy was cleansed!"

I smiled. I knew Jesus had this power, and was pleased Dovev had witnessed it. "Will that be in your report to the Sanhedrin?"

Dovev shook his head. "I would, under another circumstance, tell them everything. But after Jesus healed the man, he told him to tell no one, but to go and show himself to the priests, and offer the gift that Moses commanded, for a testimony to them. I hesitate to report that which was intended to be a private matter."

"No, you are right, Dovev, that would not be appropriate. But I am glad you saw what happened."

"As am I, Joseph. As am I."

Jesus continued to go about preaching, and we kept hearing word of his miracles and healings. His ministry was full-time – he traveled constantly, going about doing good and teaching great truths to those who would listen.

We understood the importance of his mission, but we all missed him dearly – especially his wife and daughters.

But mostly I worried for his safety. I did not voice this concern to his family, but I did speak to Mary as we walked one evening along the quiet streets of the city near our home.

"Mary, Dovev tells me that the Sanhedrin is becoming very . . . displeased with Jesus. They frequently discuss ways to ensnare him – they want to make it look like he is behaving contrary to the law. I worry for him."

"I know, Joseph. I worry, too. They are very powerful men. They do not look well upon any threat to that power. And I know they see Jesus as a threat. We must have faith that God will protect him."

I just nodded. Inside, I felt like crying out. I had spent my whole adult life being so protective of the Messiah . . . even rushing off to Egypt to save his life. Now, I felt helpless, and I felt a great foreboding regarding the political rumblings among Jerusalem's elite. But there was no point in making Mary a party to my fears. I took a deep breath. "Yes. I am sure it will all work out."

We arrived home from our walk to find Peter already there, speaking with the children.

"Hail, Peter!"

"Joseph, thank you for your hospitality. I was just telling the children about what happened yesterday at my home."

"Oh? What was that?"

"Jesus came, and he saw my wife's mother lying on her bed, sick and feverish. And he took hold of her hand, and the fever left her! She arose from her bed and ministered to us." Tears filled Peter's eyes. "It was magnificent!"

I smiled. Perhaps, if Jesus could so readily heal others, I need not worry so much about his well-being.

"And then," Peter continued, "in my neighborhood that evening, they brought to Jesus many who were possessed with devils – and he cast out the spirits with his word, and healed all who were sick." Peter reached for me and clasped my forearm with his strong grip. "Joseph, I am deeply moved to exclaim that it is a fulfillment of that which was spoken by Esaias the prophet, when he said 'he himself took our infirmities, and bore our sicknesses.' Jesus is truly the Savior!"

Again, I felt comforted with these words. Surely, Jesus is the Messiah. And so, why should I worry? What could happen to him?

Several weeks passed, and Jesus became very well known – in fact, I did not know anybody who had not heard of his sermons and his healings. Everyone who came to the carpentry shop asked me about him. With his great works, and his astonishing teachings – his followers multiplied quickly across the region. So many people hungered and thirsted after the pure message he expounded with authority.

It warmed my heart to finally see him fulfilling his destiny and blessing so many lives.

Yet, the more attention he received, the more I worried. Day by day, the hair of my head and beard began to turn gray. Mary told me she was concerned for me; I would not eat very much, and I could not sleep at night. Sometimes my heart hurt physically, with stabbing pains that brought me to my knees. My concern for Jesus kept growing more intense, weakening my body, but not my faith.

And a visit from Dovev, bearing awful news, did not help at all.

We sat in the corner of the main room of the house, and he spoke in a whisper.

"Joseph . . . Joseph, this is very troubling. I have tried to persuade some of the others to abandon their attempts to ensnare Jesus, but the Sanhedrin is very determined. They will not back down. They have devised a plan." He gulped. "A wicked plot."

My stomach twisted into a tight knot. "Tell me, what is it?"

"From what they have said, I believe they . . . they are going to publicly accuse Jesus of crimes against our laws and against the laws of our Roman occupiers. They intend to bring him to trial – an unrighteous trial with lying witnesses. Joseph – they are going to bring great harm to Jesus!"

I felt a sudden, sharp pain in my heart.

My head felt like it was going to burst open. I could not catch my breath.

I clutched at my chest, and fell toward the floor.

Everything went black and silent.

I did not dream.

I awoke in my own sleeping chamber.

My limbs were so weak; I could not lift my hands.

At my bedside, my lovely Mary watched over

me, caressing my forehead.

"Joseph," she whispered. "You are awake."

I tried to speak, but one side of my face felt numb and immobile. My words came out slurred. "Mary. Mary, what has happened?"

"Your heart is failing you, my husband. You must rest."

Suddenly, Dovev's revelation came back to me. "Mary," I struggled, "J-Jesus!" My voice was so weak – I was screaming out on the inside, but only a hoarse whisper escaped my dry lips. "They are going . . . to . . . to kill . . ."

"Shhhhh," she whispered. "You must rest. It will all be all right, Joseph."

I wanted to speak – I *had* to speak. But I could not.

I closed my eyes for a moment, and suddenly I felt lighter than air.

"Joseph?" Mary said, alarmed. She placed her face next to my parted lips. "Joseph? Dovev! Get Luke! He is not breathing! *Dovev!*"

My stomach lurched, as if I'd slipped and fallen from a rooftop; only I did not fall. Instead, I suddenly found myself looking down at my own body. It was very disorienting.

And the deep, heavy pain in my chest was gone.

As my mind raced in an attempt to understand this most unusual experience, a voice from behind startled me.

"Joseph."

I turned, just as Mary leaned over my twin on the bed, and began to quietly weep.

"You!" I whispered, awestruck by the figure before me.

"Yes, Joseph, it is I, Gabriel. It has been, for you, many years since we spoke."

"What – what is this thing that is happening?" I asked, staggering toward the angel and glancing back at the scene of grief taking place in my own bed chamber. Mary, Dovev and Luke, and Mary the wife of Jesus, and all the children had gathered around . . . the other me.

"You are no longer among the living," Gabriel said calmly, as if saying such a thing were the most natural thing in the world. "You have joined us, now. It is good to see you on this side of the veil again. You don't remember yet, but you will. Joseph, I am not just a messenger who has delivered God's word to you a few times – I am your Escort. For we have known one another for a very long time – from long before your mortal life or mine. There was a time we fought side by side as brothers – in a great war – as the strongest of allies and the best of friends."

I was stupefied.

Dead?

And Gabriel an old friend?

"You will understand all of this in due time, my friend. Come, it is best not to linger here at this time – you can do nothing to comfort them right now."

Gabriel reached out his hand and grasped my forearm gently. His warm touch tingled slightly.

I tore my gaze away from my beautiful, beloved wife and family, all of whom were now crying great tears of sorrow . . . and Gabriel led me away . . .

CHAPTER XIII – THE OTHER SIDE OF THE VEIL

Time.

It moved very differently in this realm.

It flew like a great falcon, rushing forward as a blur – and it stood still as the morning air in spring time. And we seemed to move from place to place with no effort. I could see nothing and everything at once.

It was confusing.

But Gabriel helped me. He stayed by my side and explained everything, a little at a time – thoughtfully listening to my questions and providing answers that made sense.

"Why," I asked after several moments that may have been lifetimes, "why am I still on the earth, able to walk around and see everything as I could before I – before I died?"

The word "died" rung in my ears, sounded hollow. Sounded false – as if the whole concept of death were some kind of illusion, or a story told to little children.

"The spirit world inhabits the same space as that of the living," said Gabriel. "It just exists differently. The veil that separates the living from the dead does not divide two different places – only two different perspectives. And from *that* perspective," he said, pointing to a man tending his fishing nets along the shore, "only the living can be seen. But for us, we observe both."

I pondered. "But – if I can see both, where are all the other people who have passed away? I only see you and I."

"That is correct," Gabriel said, "for now, you will only see them – the living – and us. Later when your work upon the earth is finished, your eyes will be opened to see much more – such as the spirits of your fathers. Normally, those who die are greeted by their closest family. But I was sent instead – to help prepare you for your work."

"Wait – my work upon the earth is not finished? Oh, mighty angel, I am dead! What more work can I do?"

"You shall see," Gabriel said. "Come. Jesus and his apostles have entered into that ship over there. Let us follow.

We walked toward the deep blue waters that twinkled with sunlight. I could smell the salt air – a strange sensation, since I seemed to be somehow separate from the physical world – and yet more at one with it than ever.

We entered into the ship. Nobody could see us, but for a moment, I thought Jesus was aware of my presence . . . but I was only having hopeful thoughts. The ship set out, and after only a short time at sea there arose a great tempest, and the ship was covered with the waves. But Jesus was asleep, resting soundly from his busy day of walking, preaching, and healing.

As the storm grew more violent, his apostles came to him, and awoke him, saying, "Lord, save us: we're going to die!"

And Jesus said to them, "Why are you so afraid, you of little faith?"

Then he arose, and raised his hand with authority, and rebuked the winds and the sea; and suddenly there was a great calm upon the waters.

And the men of the ship all marveled, saying, "What manner of man is this, that even the winds and the sea obey him?"

"I know what manner of man he is," I said, knowing they could not hear me. "He is the Son of God – the very Christ. He *made* this world – of course it obeys his command."

The next thing I knew, the whole scene had changed before my eyes. We had now come to the other side of the water, and were in a place called Gergesenes.

In this place there was a man who was demonically possessed. He was naked, and wild, and he lived among the tombs. He was so fierce that no one could even pass by the area.

As Jesus approached, the man cried out, saying, "What have we to do with you, Jesus, the Son of God? Have you come here to torment us before the appointed hour?"

"What is your name?" asked Jesus with perfect serenity and kindness.

"My name is Legion, for we are many."

Jesus looked at him, and the evil spirits that possessed him seemed to know what was about to happen. Seeing a herd of swine up on the hillside, the man said, "Please, if you cast us out, let us go into that herd of swine. Anything is better than the torment of not having a body. Anything."

Jesus looked at the man with pity in his eyes, and said to the evil spirits, "Go."

When they came out, they went into the herd of swine: and the whole herd of swine ran violently down the steep hill into the sea, and they died there in the waters.

The keepers of the swine ran away, and went into the town, and told everything that had happened. Soon, the townspeople came out to see what had happened to the possessed man. When they saw him, instead of being impressed and glad for the healed man, they asked Jesus to leave the area.

"The loss of some pigs seems a small price to pay for the healing of that poor man," I said to Gabriel.

"Yet they drive Jesus out," said Gabriel. "Men are often hard-hearted and blind. You will see more of that."

The healed man, now perfectly normal again, clothed and able to speak, no longer cutting himself with stones or doing any such wild thing, came to Jesus as he was departing into the ship.

"Master, may I stay with you? I will journey wherever you go."

"No, return to your friends and family, and tell them what great things the Lord has done for you –

that I had compassion on you."

The man obeyed and went his way, telling everyone he saw about his miraculous recovery.

A moment later, so it seemed, Gabriel and I were elsewhere, in the middle of the day. We stood and watched as Jesus entered into another ship. We boarded as well, and in time we passed over to the other side of the waters.

I watched as the people brought a man – a very sick man – to Jesus. He was lying on a bed and appeared to have the palsy. Because there were so many people there to see Jesus, the men had to remove parts of the roof to lower the sick man down near Jesus.

Jesus seemed moved by the faith of these people as they went through great efforts to bring the man to him. He said to the sick man, "Son, be of good cheer; your sins are forgiven you."

I watched as some of the scribes in the crowd looked at each other with astonishment.

But Jesus, it seemed, could read their thoughts. "Why do you think evil in your hearts, and believe that I blaspheme? Is it easier to say, 'Your sins are forgiven you;' or to say, 'Arise, and walk?' But that you may know that the Son of Man has power on earth to forgive sins . . ."

And then he turned to the sick man. "Arise, take up your bed, and go to your house."

The crowd murmured in shock as the man arose, and departed to his own home, fully healed.

Without saying more, Jesus left and walked

through the streets, where he came to a man who was doing his job as a tax collector.

Jesus simply walked up to him and said, "Matthew, follow me."

The man arose from his seat and followed him immediately, leaving his task behind.

"Who is that?" I asked Gabriel.

"Jesus is now going about and calling the remainder of his quorum – the twelve who will be his apostles."

"That *tax collector* will be an apostle? A leader in Jesus' kingdom?"

"There are all kinds of men who are worthy for such a calling," Gabriel said. "Do not forget, it was only a lowly carpenter who was called to be the earthly father of the Savior of mankind."

I nodded, humbled and corrected.

The next thing I knew, we were in the house of Matthew. Jesus was there with his apostles, sitting and eating with many publicans and people well-known for their sinful way of living.

Then Dovev entered, along with several of the Pharisees. The Pharisees looked upon the scene, then said to Jesus' apostles, rather than directly addressing Jesus, "Why does your Master eat with publicans and sinners?"

Jesus heard their derisive remark – less of a question than an accusation. He turned to them and said, "Those who are whole are in no need of a physician – it is the sick who need help. Think about that. For I have not come to call the righteous to repentance, but sinners."

Again, everything seemed to change before my eyes, and we were somewhere else. I recognized the street, only a short walk from my carpentry shop. Jesus was speaking with some people – disciples of John the Baptist, when a man I knew to be Jairus, a ruler in the city, approached and fell at Jesus' feet, saying, "My daughter – she has fallen ill, and died! But I know that if you, Jesus, can just come lay your hand upon her, she will live."

Jesus placed his hand on Jairus' shoulder, to comfort him, then followed him to his home, with his apostles walking behind.

As they walked, a crowd quickly gathered and followed, hoping to witness a miracle. And as that crowd passed through a narrow street, a woman came behind Jesus and touched the hem of his robe. I wondered why she would do that.

"Watch," said Gabriel, aware of my unspoken question.

Jesus stopped, and turned around, saying, "Who touched my robe?"

The woman, a bright gleam in her eyes, said, "Master, it was I. I have been sick for twelve years with a blood illness. The doctors can not heal me. When I saw you, I thought that if I could just touch your clothing, I could be healed."

"Daughter," he said kindly, "be of good comfort. Your faith has made you whole."

As Jesus continued on with his group, the woman began to weep great tears of joy.

Eventually, Jesus reached the house of Jairus, and saw the friends and family of Jairus mourning over the loss of the little girl.

"The girl is not dead, only sleeping," he said.

But the mourners laughed bitterly at his words, knowing full well that the girl was dead.

Jesus looked to his apostles, and they helped clear the way so Jesus could get through to the house. Once inside, Jesus came to the girl's beside, and took her by the hand, and she arose.

All those outside who had been mourning, and did not believe the words of Jesus when he was on his way in, had a serious change of heart when he came out, along with the living daughter of Jairus.

Amazed, they went out from the house and spread the word of what had happened across the land.

Gabriel and I moved on again, and over and over we watched as Jesus healed blind men, cast out devils from others, and was scorned by the Pharisees for his miraculous acts of goodness. They even went so far as to say he was working under the power of the devil – a foolish charge, given that he was doing good wherever he went.

I heard him say to a lowly multitude, "Come to me, all you who are burdened with work and sorrows – and I will give you rest. Take my yoke upon you, and learn of me; for I am meek and lowly in heart, and you will find rest for your souls. For my yoke is easy, and my burden is light."

"His burden is light?" I asked Gabriel. "How is his burden light? He bears the weight of the world."

"Exactly," said Gabriel. "He bears the weight for everyone – so when they yoke themselves to him, he carries the load, making the burden appear light."

We moved on, and watched more healing and teaching.

At some point, perhaps it was the very

beginning – it is so hard to place, as if time had no meaning – I asked Gabriel a question that had seemed to be bothering me for years. Or moments.

"Gabriel, why are you showing me all these things?"

"Training, of course."

"Training? For what?"

"You shall see, Joseph. Patience."

We continued to glide through time, and from place to place, moving effortlessly.

At last, Jesus had called all his apostles – twelve of them – and he blessed them and laid hands on their heads, and set them apart from the world, giving them their commissions. He taught them and gave them power against unclean spirits – the power to cast them out – and also the power to heal all kinds of sickness and diseases.

What a blessing to have such priesthood power to be able to bless the lives of others!

Jesus commanded them, saying, "Do not go teach the Gentiles or the Samaritans yet, but instead go to the lost sheep of the house of Israel, and as you go, preach, saying, 'The kingdom of heaven is at hand.' Heal the sick, cleanse the lepers, raise the dead, cast out devils – all the things you have seen me do. As you have freely received, freely give."

He instructed them to set aside their temporal concerns while on their mission. "Do not worry about carrying money as you go out and preach, and do not worry about clothing. You are in the service of your God – that is all you need to know. All else will take care of itself."

Next, he gave counsel regarding how their

message is received.

"When you come into someone's house, show respect. And if the house is worthy, let your peace come upon it; but if it is not worthy, let your peace return to you. And whoever will not receive you or hear your words, when you depart out of that house or city, shake off the dust of your feet. And know this: it will be more tolerable for the land of Sodom and Gomorrah, in the day of judgment, than for that city that has rejected my gospel. I send you forth as sheep in the midst of wolves – so you need to be wise as serpents, yet harmless as doves. But know this: you will be persecuted – even punished – for following me and spreading my teachings. Are you ready for that?"

The apostles all nodded; some said, "Yes, Master."

"But when they deliver you up to the rulers," he continued, "take no thought for what to say – for it will be given to you in that same hour what you should speak, by the power of the Holy Ghost."

"Master," asked James, "what will they do to us? Will they kill us for preaching?"

"Many men will hate you because of me, but if you endure to the end, you will be saved. Do not fear those who kill the body, but are not able to kill the soul – but rather fear those who are able to destroy both soul and body. But take comfort: your Father in Heaven will watch over you – is he not aware of the fall of a sparrow? He knows you perfectly, even the number of hairs on your head! And you, my friends, are of far more worth than sparrows – you are His sons. If you testify of me to men, I will testify in your behalf to my Father in

Heaven. But if you deny me before men, I will deny you before my Father. You must put God and His Kingdom first above all else – even your own families. This is a time to decide which side you are on."

"Master," said Phillip, "we are on your side, to the end."

Jesus nodded approvingly. "Lose your life in service of the kingdom, and you will find your life."

My world swirled around me again, and we were next traveling with Jesus and his apostles. I did not know the season in which I found myself – but somehow I knew it was the Sabbath day.

As Jesus walked, his apostles murmured that they were hungry, and began to pick ears of corn along the way and eat them.

But they came to some Pharisees, who immediately saw it as an opportunity to criticize Jesus.

"Look – your disciples do that which is not lawful to do upon the Sabbath day."

Jesus answered them and said, "Have you not read what David did, when he and those with him were hungry? How he entered into the house of God, and ate the shewbread, which was not lawful for him to eat – in fact, not lawful for anyone but the priests? Or have you not read in the law, how on the Sabbath days the priests in the temple break the Sabbath, and are blameless? I say to you that in this place is one greater than the temple. For the

Son of Man is Lord even of the Sabbath day."

The stupefied Pharisees simply stepped aside without a word as Jesus and his apostles walked past and entered their synagogue. As soon as Jesus was inside the high walls of the holy building, he saw a man whose hand was withered. Seeing another opportunity to trap Jesus, the Pharisees, who had followed him inside, asked him, "Is it lawful to heal on the Sabbath day?"

Jesus answered them with a peaceful countenance and words of pure wisdom and reason. "What man is there among you with a sheep that has fallen into a pit on the Sabbath day, would not lay hold on it, and lift it out? How much then is a man better than a sheep? Thus it is lawful to do well on the Sabbath day."

And then he said to the man, "Stretch your hand forth." And the man stretched it forth; and it was restored whole, like the other hand.

But did those Pharisees fall to their knees and praise Jesus? No. Instead, they left, angered.

"How can they be angry?" I asked. "Jesus just healed a man – a miracle! Do they not care?"

"They care more about their power," Gabriel said. "They care about using the law to maintain that power, not about the whole reason the law exists – that man may become more like God, through love and faith and good works, through the example of Christ the Lord."

"It is sad," I said. "They are so blind."

"It gets worse," Gabriel lamented.

"Worse?"

"Yes. Worse."

#

Suddenly, I found that Gabriel and I were in the Pharisees' secret meeting chambers.

It was a small room with a low ceiling and flaming sconces on the walls. In the center of the room were two long tables at which the leaders sat to discuss their hidden matters.

I spotted my friend Dovev, sitting near the door. He looked older than the last time I had seen him, though surely only a few days, maybe weeks had passed. Or perhaps it had been two or three years.

The Pharisees were counseling with each other in the flickering light. Seeking ways to destroy Jesus.

"We can cross him – get him to speak against the law," one whispered menacingly.

"That should not take much – his words drip with blasphemy at every turn," said another.

"Then we can have him condemned," said a third. "And get the Romans to crucify him."

"No!" I shouted, silent and invisible to these men. They were completely oblivious to my presence. To my pain.

I tried in vain once more. *"No!"*

The sconce nearest me flickered.

As I listened to the men continue to plot against Jesus, tears formed in my eyes. "Why, Gabriel? Why do they want to kill my son? To condemn the Son of God?"

"They have lost their way, Joseph. In the name of keeping the law and upholding righteousness, they have closed their eyes to the intent of the law. Now, they only care about their power to enforce the law – and they have hardened their hearts to the truth Jesus speaks and shows them. They see him as a threat, nothing else."

"But he is not a threat! He would harm no one! He has come to save all who would come unto him."

"They do not see it that way, Joseph."

We were once again brought to another time and place.

Jesus was once again in Galilee, and the people brought him a man possessed with a devil, who was both blind and dumb. Jesus healed him immediately – the man could now see and speak. All the people were amazed, but the Pharisees scoffed and said, "Of course he can cast out devils – because he is using the power of Beelzebub, the prince of the devils."

This really incensed me. "How can they say such a thing? Do they really believe that?"

Gabriel, calm as ever, replied, "Perhaps they have lied to themselves long enough that they do believe it. But more likely they are just stirring up trouble, trying to dissuade the people from following Jesus."

Jesus said, "Every kingdom divided against itself is brought to desolation; and every city or house divided against itself will not stand. And if Satan casts out Satan, he is divided against himself; so how would his kingdom stand? And if I, by Beelzebub, cast out devils, by whom do your children cast them out? But if I cast out devils by the Spirit of God, then the kingdom of God is come unto you."

The logic was confounding.

Then, he uttered challenging words, intended for the Pharisees and for all who could hear: "He who is not with me . . . is against me."

The Pharisees, rather than answer, began speaking quietly among themselves, and turned and walked away.

"Can I see my family?" I asked Gabriel.

"Your family? To what end?"

"I – I just want to see how they are doing. To make sure all is well. As well as it can be, with me gone."

"Joseph, there is still much more for you to see of Jesus' ministry. But yes, we may go see your family. Briefly."

A moment later, I was standing in my home.

Mary sat with my sons Benjamin and Joses, talking quietly. The boys had grown some. Dovev was there, too.

"Mary," Dovev said, "This past year, it has weighed so heavily on my heart. I feel responsible. Had I not told Joseph of the simmering plots of the Sanhedrin, his heart would not have failed him. I feel I have failed as a friend."

Mary shook her head. "Of course not, Dovev. Do not think that. It is not your fault – you did the right thing in warning Joseph. God has his reasons for taking him home – reasons we cannot know right now. But it will all be made known one day.

Please, stop carrying this burden."

"She is always so kind," I said to Gabriel. "Wait – did he say it has been a year since my death?"

"You are observing the one year point, yes," said Gabriel. "But as you have likely noticed, time is different here."

"Indeed," I said. "I cannot make sense of it."

"You will become adjusted," Gabriel assured me. "For now, are you satisfied that all is well at your home?"

"Yes," I said, "I am satisfied. I do hope Dovev stops blaming himself, though."

"We must return to your training, now," Gabriel said, taking me by the arm and leading me out of the house.

We stepped outside into the bright light of day – but we were not outside my home, but in the midst of a town square. Jesus was once again teaching the people – and as usual, there were Pharisees present.

"Whoever speaks against the Holy Ghost," Jesus said, "it will not be forgiven him, not in this world, or in the world to come. Every idle word that men speak, they will account for in the day of judgment. For by your words will you be justified, and by your words will you be condemned."

The scribes and Pharisees asked Jesus for a sign, trying once again to ensnare him.

Jesus answered, "An evil and adulterous generation seeks after a sign; and there will no sign be given to it, but the sign of the prophet Jonah. 'For as Jonah was three days and three nights in the whale's belly; so shall the Son of Man be three days and three nights in the heart of the earth.' The sign, therefore, has already been given – if you know your scriptures."

I turned to Gabriel. "What does that mean? Three days and nights in the earth?"

"You shall see in due time," Gabriel said.

"I do not like the sound of it," I said. "I fear for Jesus."

Gabriel looked at me, as if in disbelief himself. "Joseph – how is it you have seen all you have seen – conversed with me in your life, and now travel and learn with me in death – yet you still struggle with your faith?"

"I apologize. It is not that I do not have faith – for I do. It is just that Jesus – he is my son. I know he is God's son – but I delivered him into the world with my own hands, held him as a babe, watched over and protected him, taught him what I could, raised him up. I simply have so much love for him – it breaks my heart to think that anything bad would ever happen to him."

"Then you will have a very difficult time with some of the things I am yet to show you."

Before I could consider these words, everything changed once more. The next place we went was Galilee. Jesus was talking with the people inside a house, and I saw Mary, James, Joses and Benjamin waiting to speak with him outside.

One of the people said to Jesus, "Master, your mother and your brothers are standing outside – they want to speak with you."

But Jesus replied, "Who is my mother? And who are my brothers?" He stretched out his hand toward his apostles, and said, "Look, here are my mother and my brothers! For whoever does the will of my Father in Heaven, that person is my brother, and sister, and mother."

"He disowns his own family?" I said to Gabriel. "I thought we would be a family forever."

"No, Joseph, no. He loves his family. And you can be a family forever. He is trying to teach an important lesson. Yes, you and Mary and his whole family – brothers and sisters – as well as his own wife and daughters – are precious and are his family. But in the Kingdom of God, all who are obedient to the Father are brothers and sisters in Jesus – a different kind of family, and one of great importance. His family encompasses the whole human creation – as does his love."

"I see," I said, starting to realize the immensity of it all. It seemed there were so many things that Jesus had taught me while I was in the flesh, that I *thought* I understood at the time; but now, I saw, my understanding had been a mere shadow of things as they really are.

We shifted again, and this time, I seemed less disoriented. I was able to tell that we had not moved far through time or space. Perhaps I was actually beginning to become accustomed to this new reality.

Here, Jesus taught the people in their synagogue, and the people were astonished at his words. Someone said, "How does this man have such wisdom, and do these mighty works? Is he not the carpenter's son? Is not his mother called Mary? And his brethren, James, and Joses, and Simon, and Judas? And his sisters, are they not all part of our community? His family is a good family, but how did he come to have such great knowledge and power?"

"Yes," said another, "how is it this man of humble background has such authority?"

Jesus said to them, "A prophet is not without honor, except in his own country, and in his own house."

And he left, without doing any further miracles there, because they did not have sufficient faith.

"I do not understand," I said. "Why would those who know that he is from a good family doubt him? Why do they question his authority, just because they have known him and his family since before his ministry?"

"Faith is an interesting thing, Joseph," said Gabriel. "Unfortunately, for some, familiarity is a stumbling block to their belief. Some expect the Messiah to be exotic, to come suddenly from an unknown place, to swoop in and astound. Despite the astounding words and works of Jesus, they have difficulty believing that such greatness could come from among their own people – from a humble carpenter's family. They rely too much on their imagined ideas of how greatness appears, how it is achieved, what it *looks* like in their own imaginations. He simply does not match the way they see the Messiah in their minds."

It stung a little to realize that this inability of theirs to see things as they really are mirrored my own lack of understanding. While in life, I had believed that I knew so much – that my knowledge and perspective were clear – especially as I was aided by parenting the Savior. Now I saw that even with all my advantages, I had fallen short in my progress.

Yet now, all was so much clearer.

The next movement definitely disoriented me. I had no idea where we were.

But I did recognize the man before us: although he looked terribly mistreated, I could see that he was John the Baptist.

"Where are we?" I asked Gabriel.

"We are in a wicked place, my friend: the palace of Herod the Tetrarch."

"Why?" And what has become of John?"

"Herod has imprisoned John, because John spoke a truth he did not want to hear. But he has not put him to death, for he fears a backlash from John's many followers, for they know him to be a prophet. To avoid rebellion, he keeps John locked away like an animal."

Next, we were upstairs from the dungeon, amidst revelry – food and dancing.

"What is happening here?"

Gabriel explained, "It is Herod's birthday celebration."

I saw the daughter of Herodias dancing before the men, and saw that Herod was pleased.

"Such wonderful dancing!" he exclaimed. "I do swear, I will give that girl anything she would ask for. Anything."

Without hesitation, the impudent girl said, "Give me John Baptist's head on a plate."

The music stopped.

"What?" asked the king, taken aback.

"His head. On a plate. Now." The girl glanced to

her mother, who gave an approving nod.

"Well, I did swear an oath," said Herod.

"No!" I cried out. But nobody could hear me. "Gabriel, this must be stopped! What can we do?"

Gabriel had tears in his eyes. "Nothing, Joseph. Men are given their agency, and we cannot take that away. They will use that agency for good or evil, but as much as it pains us, as much as it pains God, he will never – never – take that away."

I watched as Herod sent away the men from the table to go and do the awful deed.

Down below, in the cavernous dungeon, I heard a brief scream, and knew it was over.

A tear dropped from Gabriel's eye. The king winced, then quickly regained his composure. The lips of Herodias and her daughter formed serpentine smiles.

I felt a heavy pain in my heart as they brought in John's head on a silver plate, still freshly bleeding, his eyes closed, and handed it to the girl, who promptly delivered it to her monstrous mother.

Shortly after, John's followers came and took his body to bury it.

A moment later, Gabriel and I were elsewhere, near the seashore, and we watched as those same followers approached Jesus.

"Master," one of them solemnly said, "it is a dark day. We bear terrible news. John the Baptist is dead. Herod the Tetrarch had him beheaded. We have buried his body already."

Jesus' face flashed with pain, and then he simply nodded.

Then he got up and walked away.

"He wants to be alone, to mourn," I said,

remembering the many times growing up that Jesus would move apart from others to ponder important things. "This was his beloved cousin – murdered – a man Jesus said was even greater than a prophet. He must wish to have some privacy."

I watched him travel by ship, then walk into a deserted place, far from others, and sit down and watch the ships on the distant waters.

But he did not have solitude for long. His followers had tracked his movements and were walking, in droves, to reach him.

Jesus stood, and moved toward the crowd that was forming.

"What is he doing?" I asked.

"Look," said Gabriel, "he is moved with compassion for these followers."

We watched as Jesus healed their sick, one by one.

I was amazed. How did Jesus cope with this awful, sad news of John's death? He jumped immediately into service and helped others. I knew there was a great lesson in this.

Jesus continued to minister to the people's needs until it was evening.

When the sun had dipped low in the sky, his apostles came to him. Peter said, "Master, it is late, and we are in a barren place. We should send the multitude away, so they may go into the villages, and buy themselves some food to eat."

"They do not need to go away," Jesus said. "Give them food."

"But we have here only five loaves, and two fish," said Thomas.

"Bring them here to me."

They brought Jesus the meager food portions, and then Jesus commanded the crowd to sit down on the grass. Then he took the five loaves, and the two fish, and looking up to heaven, he blessed them with a prayer, and he broke the bread, gave it to his apostles, and the disciples in turn gave it to the crowd.

Somehow, every one of the people there got some bread, and ate it, and was filled. When they collected up the remaining bread pieces, it filled twelve baskets.

"There must be five thousand men – plus women and children, here," I said, marveling. "A miracle!"

Gabriel grinned. "Our God does truly love all his children."

Jesus then sent his apostles to return by ship, and he sent the crowd away. Then he hiked up into a nearby mountain, to pray, alone.

Instead of following him to watch him pray, Gabriel and I went with the apostles on the ship. Later that night – when it was nearly morning – I looked out in the misty false dawn, and saw a figure coming toward the ship, upon the water.

Pater saw the same thing. A man *walking* on the water.

"It is a spirit," he cried out in fear.

But the voice of Jesus, calm and clear, immediately answered, "Be of good cheer, it is me. Do not be afraid."

"See how he comforted them immediately, not letting them fear a moment longer?" said Gabriel.

"Yes," I said.

Peter then said, "Lord, if it is you, ask me to

come out to you on the water."

"Come."

Peter immediately climbed down the side of the ship. Without hesitation, he stepped out onto the water, and he walked upon it, just as Jesus was doing, making his way to the Messiah. But when the wind came up strong, he feared – and he started to sink.

"Lord, save me!"

Jesus immediately stretched out his hand, and caught him, and said to him, "Oh, you of little faith, why did you doubt?"

"Again," I said, "he immediately reached out and helped him. Ask for his help, and he helps you."

"You are learning," Gabriel said.

Jesus carefully guided Peter to the ship, holding his hand, helping him to walk on the water. When they were aboard the ship, the wind stopped, and all those on the ship came and worshipped Jesus, saying, "You are the Son of God, indeed!"

Next, we were at a synagogue in Capernaum.

Jesus had called together a crowd, and was once again teaching. I was surprised to see Dovev in the crowd. Either he was on assignment from the Sanhedrin, or he was simply there to learn for himself.

"Hear, and understand," Jesus said, "It is not that which goes into the mouth that defiles a man, but that which comes out of his mouth – that is what defiles a man."

A man in the crowd turned to Dovev and said, "Do you hear this, what this man is saying in defiance of the Pharisees?"

"Yes," said Dovev, "he has mentioned that to me before – some few years ago. The subject came up at supper."

"You know this man?" said the man, surprised.

"Yes. I am a friend of his family. At first, when he said these things, I was taken aback. But he is right. What he says is true."

The man, shocked to hear a member of the Sanhedrin agree with Jesus, walked away with a perplexed look on his face.

"Ah, good man, Dovev, good man," I said, pleased to see my old friend taking a stand. I wondered what his peers would think if they found out that he had defended Jesus in a public setting.

"Joseph," said Gabriel, "I am now going to take you to witness something quite extraordinary."

In a flash, we were atop a very high mountain, surrounded by craggy boulders and small, dry plants. The sky was darkening, and the wind blew steadily from the west.

Jesus was there, along with Peter, James, and John.

Jesus stood apart from them a few paces, and suddenly, a light grew all around him. His face shined, and his clothing was as white as noonday sunlight.

Then two men appeared, and were talking with

Jesus.

"Who is that?" I asked.

"Moses. And Elias."

"Can the apostles see them, too – or only us?"

"What you are seeing is called a transfiguration, Joseph. Yes, Moses and Elias are here in our realm – but Jesus, and his three apostles there – they can see them. They have been transfigured – their bodies and minds altered so that they can observe the fullness of reality, including that which lies beyond the veil."

"So . . . if they were to look over here, they would see us?"

Gabriel smiled. "Yes. But they won't. They are receiving instruction now."

"Lord," Peter said to Jesus, "it is good for us to be here. If you want, let us make three tabernacles here; one for you, and one for Moses, and one for Elias."

Before he was done speaking, a bright cloud overshadowed them, and a voice came out of the cloud, saying, "This is my beloved Son, in whom I am well pleased; hear him."

When the apostles heard it, they fell on their faces, and were very afraid. Jesus came and touched them, and said, "Arise, and do not be afraid."

The apostles looked up then, but now they saw only Jesus.

Stunned and amazed, they returned back down the mountain with Jesus. When they reached the bottom, Jesus said, "Do not discuss with anyone what you just witnessed. Not until the Son of Man has risen again from the dead."

I turned to Gabriel. "Risen from the dead? I do not understand."

"You will."

A moment later, we were in Galilee once again, and Jesus was talking to his apostles.

He said, "The Son of Man will be betrayed into the hands of men, and they will kill him, and the third day he will be raised again."

As the apostles grieved at hearing this announcement, I said to Gabriel, "Now I understand. It is what Dovev was warning me about on the day I died. They are going to murder my son."

And I turned away and wept.

Gabriel put his arm around my shoulder and led me away. The scene changed all around us, and I found that we were in a street.

"Now," said Gabriel, as I wiped away the tears, "we will watch as Jesus instructs his apostles. Pay close attention – you will need to know and understand all these principles."

I wondered what he meant by that – what was ahead for me.

I focused in and listened.

"Who is the greatest in the kingdom of heaven?" Andrew asked Jesus.

Jesus called a little child to him and had the boy stand in the middle of the group. "I tell you with certainty, that unless you are converted, and become as little children, you will not enter into the kingdom of heaven. Whoever humbles himself like this little child is greatest in the kingdom of heaven. And whoever will receive one such little child in my name, receives me. But whoever offends one of these little ones who believe in me – he would be better off if a millstone were hung around his neck and he were drowned in the depths of the sea."

Strong words. And very true.

He continued. "The Son of Man has come to save that which was lost. Consider this: if a man has a hundred sheep, and one of them goes astray, does he not leave the ninety-nine, and go into the mountains, and seek after the one that has gone astray?"

The apostles nodded thoughtfully.

"And if he finds it, you know that he rejoices more over that sheep, than of the ninety-nine that did not go astray. Likewise, it is not the will of your Heavenly Father that even one of these little ones should perish."

He moved to a different topic. He stood and placed his hands upon Peter's head.

"I now give to you the sealing power. Whatever you bind on earth will be bound in heaven, and whatever you loose on earth will be loosed in heaven. This is a powerful matter. Use good judgment. Also, if two of you agree regarding any request of your Heavenly Father, it will be done. For where two or three are gathered together in my name, I will be there also."

As Jesus moved to the others to place his hands on their heads, Peter spoke. "Lord, how many times should I forgive my brother when he sins against me – seven times?"

"I say to you," Jesus answered, "Not seven

times, but seventy times seven."

Again, he was establishing a higher law.

And he taught a parable.

"The kingdom of heaven is like a certain king, who came to collect debts from his subjects. And one of these servants owed him ten thousand talents. But he had no means by which to pay, so the king commanded that the man and his wife and children be sold into slavery to pay the debt. And the man fell down, and worshipped the king, begging him to have patience, and said that he would pay all that was owed. Seeing this, the king had compassion, and freed the man, and forgave the debt. But the same servant then went out and found one of his friends who owed him just one hundred pence, and he seized him by the throat and demanded the other pay his debt. The other man dropped to his knees and pleaded for patience, but the man would not have compassion, and he threw him into prison until the debt was paid. When the king heard of this, he had the first man brought to him once again, and he said, 'You wicked man! I forgave you all that debt, because you asked me. Should you not have had compassion on your friend, as I had pitied you?' And the king was angry, and had the man taken away to suffer until he paid his debt."

"I have seen people like that," I said to Gabriel. "They are treated well, then they turn around and mistreat others. It is sad."

"It is wicked," said Gabriel.

"And so shall your Father in Heaven deal with you," said Jesus. "If you do not forgive all others in your heart, you will not be forgiven."

Then a group came by, bringing with them their little children.

"Might Jesus lay his hands on them, and pray?" a woman asked.

"Not now – take them away," said Simon. "Jesus is busy now, teaching us."

"No, Simon," said Jesus, "let them come to me – for such is the kingdom of heaven."

Jesus then spent over an hour blessing the children before going on his way.

Again, things changed around me, and we were at Perea. Jesus was finishing a sermon.

A young man approached him, well-dressed in fine clothing – clearly a wealthy man.

"Good Master," he said, "what good thing should I do that I may have eternal life?"

Jesus said, "If you want eternal life, keep the commandments."

"Which commandments?"

"Do not murder, do not commit adultery, do not steal, do not lie, honor your father and your mother – and love your neighbor as yourself."

The young man smiled and said, "I have kept all these commandments since I was a child. Is there anything else I lack?"

"If you truly want to be perfect," Jesus said, "Go and sell everything you have, and give the money to the poor. Then you will have treasure in heaven. And come and follow me."

When the young man heard that instruction, he went away, his face downcast and his heart full of sorrow – for he had many valuable possessions he could not bear the thought of parting with.

Then I saw Dovev – who had once again been present for a sermon of Jesus. I hoped he was truly being converted, and that he could have a good influence on the Sanhedrin.

I watched, and listened, as Dovev approached the wealthy young man.

"Hello, friend," he said. "I am Dovev, of the Sanhedrin. Why do you look so troubled?"

"Hail, Dovev. I am Nachum." He looked down at his feet. "How can I do as the Master asks? I cannot live without all my possessions – I have worked hard for them, and I have become very accustomed to my way of life."

Dovev kindly placed his hand on the young man's shoulder and quietly said, "Friend, you cannot live *with* those things – not truly, eternally live. Give up your comforts, Nachum." Dovev smiled faintly. "Think carefully on what Jesus has said to you. He has instructed you on the means to a perfect life, and to having treasure in heaven. I can see you are a good man. Choose to be great."

The young man considered these words, and, with tears in his eyes, nodded slowly. "My heart wants to do this, but my head does not understand. I know that it is right to give alms to the poor, but how can giving away all that I have earned – everything – make me more fit for the kingdom of heaven?"

"Jesus has said that it is easier for a camel to go through the eye of the needle than for a rich man to enter into the kingdom of God," Dovev said. He considered for a moment and his mind caught hold of something he'd once heard in his travels south of Horeb. "Have you ever been to Jeroham?"

With a look of surprise at the apparently sudden change of subject, the young man said cautiously, "No. Why do you ask?"

"North of there, in some mountains, I am told there is a narrow pass known as the Eye of the Needle. It is so narrow, my friend, that you cannot pass through without dismounting your camel, unburdening it from its packs and loads, and carefully leading it through. The path is so narrow and so high in elevation that the camel must be blindfolded, so it does not scare and run madly over the cliff."

The young man frowned silently for a few moments. "Yes. Yes, I see. Humility – a willingness to leave behind the things of this world – and a willingness to be led, purely on faith." He scratched at his chin thoughtfully. "It is a hard thing the Master asks – but he certainly teaches the truth." He grinned. "I will do it."

I was amazed to see Dovev so brilliantly teaching that young man, persuading him to follow Jesus. Whether Dovev vocally opposed the Sanhedrin or not, he certainly had his own testimony of Jesus, from what I was seeing. And that made me glad.

And it made me wonder about others I loved.

Did all of my children believe?

What about the families of Jesus' apostles?

I listened once more, just as Jesus was saying, "...everyone who has forsaken houses, or brothers, or sisters, or father, or mother, or wife, or children, or lands, for my name's sake, will receive a hundredfold, and will inherit everlasting life. Many that are first will be last; and the last will be first."

This must have brought some comfort to those apostles – knowing that all they were doing would be worth it in the end. I wondered what else they would be called upon to sacrifice in the service of the Kingdom.

Would it cost them their lives?

By and by, Gabriel took us to Bethany, where a good friend of Jesus – someone known to our whole family – had just died. When Jesus arrived, Lazarus had been lying in a tomb for four days.

Many visitors had arrived to mourn with and comfort Martha and Mary, his sisters.

Martha heard from one of the visitors that Jesus was on his way, and as soon as she heard this, she ran out to meet him while Mary remained behind at the house.

"Jesus, Lord," she said, "If you had been here, my brother would not have died. I know you could have saved him – I know you have the power. But even now – I know you have the power to do anything. Anything. Whatever you ask of God, I know he will give it to you."

Jesus looked at Martha and tears welled in his eyes. I knew that he loved this family, and I could see that he was pleased with Martha's powerful faith. He gently placed his hand on her shoulder and looked her straight in the eyes. "Your brother will rise again," he said.

"I know that he will rise again in the

resurrection, at the last day," Martha said.

"I am the resurrection, and the life. He who believes in me, though he were dead, yet will he live. And whoever lives and believes in me will never die. Do you believe this?"

"Yes, Lord, I believe that you are the Christ, the Son of God, who was prophesied to come into the world."

Then she walked toward her house, and took Mary aside privately, and told her that Jesus had come. As soon as Mary heard that, she quickly went out to meet him. Jesus was not yet at Bethany, but was still in the place where Martha had met him. The people who had come to mourn with the family saw Mary go out, and assumed she was heading out to mourn at the tomb, so they followed her.

When Mary reached Jesus, she fell down at his feet. "Lord, if you had been here, my brother would not have died."

When Jesus saw her weeping, and also her visitors crying, he closed his eyes and sighed deeply – clearly touched and full of compassion.

"Where have you laid Lazarus?" he asked.

"Lord, come and see," said Mary.

When they reached the tomb, a gray stone cave, underground at the bottom of a flight of steps, Jesus stopped and wept.

"Look at how he loved him," said one of the visitors quietly.

Another said, "Could not this man, who opened the eyes of the blind, have somehow prevented Lazarus from dying?"

Jesus stepped to the stone covering the tomb

entrance.

"Take away the stone," he said.

"Lord, by this time, he will smell bad – he has been dead for four days," said Martha.

"Did I not say to you that if you would believe, you would see the glory of God?" said Jesus.

I watched from only a few paces away as four strong men took away the stone from the tomb entrance. Then Jesus lifted up his eyes, and said, "Father, I thank you that you have heard me. And I have always known that you hear me always – but I say this for the benefit of these who are here with me – that they may believe that you have sent me."

A moment of silence.

Then, with a loud voice, Jesus said, "Lazarus, come forth!"

After a moment, I heard footsteps coming from the darkness of the tomb – and then, to everyone's utter amazement, Lazarus – who had been dead – came shuffling out of the tomb! He was bound hand and foot with burial clothes, and his face was wrapped with a cloth.

"Loose him, and let him go," Jesus said to the dumbstruck crowd. Someone stepped forward cautiously and unwrapped the face of Lazarus.

Mary and Martha rushed forward and embraced their brother, who seemed a little dazed and pale, but otherwise well. He looked at Jesus, and Jesus gave him a little nod.

"Well, there must be a few more believers among this group today," I said to Gabriel.

"Indeed, Joseph. But not all. See those few men leaving?"

"Yes."

"Come, let us go see where they are going."

A moment later, we were at the meeting place of the Pharisees. Those few men who had been at the tomb of Lazarus were there now, and they were telling the Pharisees what they had seen.

Shortly after this, the chief priests and the Pharisees held a council.

"What are we supposed to do?" complained one of them. "This man is doing many miracles – even raising the dead!"

"Yes," snarled a heavy-set one seated near the head of the table. "If we leave him to do as he pleases, it will not be long before everyone believes in *Jesus*. And then do you know what will happen? The Romans will come, and they will relieve us of our power and authority! And if they feel threatened enough, perhaps they will just destroy us all!"

Then one named Caiaphas, said, "It is simple, what we should do. It is better that this one man should die, than that our whole nation be swept asunder."

To my shock, nobody objected. Instead, they took counsel together regarding how they would go about making sure that Jesus would be killed.

As they were talking, Dovev entered.

"What are you discussing?" he quietly asked one of the Pharisees seated nearest the door.

"How we can put an end to our troubles with this Jesus of Nazareth."

"Do you mean to drive him out?" Dovev asked.

"We mean to drive him to the grave," said the Pharisee.

Dovev gulped. I could see that he was

struggling mightily to refrain from doing something rash – something to defend Jesus. Something that would get him, possibly, killed as well.

These were powerful and dangerous men.

Dovev squirmed in his seat as the men devised their wicked plans. I could see he wanted to flee, but I knew he only wanted to know what was planned, so he may somehow be able to warn Jesus.

By the end of the evening, the Pharisees were smiling, Dovev was sweating, and the fate of Jesus had been decided.

The Passover was coming, and so was Jesus.

"If only he would avoid Jerusalem," I said to Gabriel as we watched him with his apostles near the village of Bethphage, near the Mount of Olives. "If he would just stay away for a while, perhaps he would be safe."

"It is not his intention to hide, or to be safe," Gabriel said. "That is not his mission."

Of course. I had to keep reminding myself that despite my desire to see Jesus safe, that was not the plan. That was not why he had come to earth.

As the group approached Bethphage, Jesus said to his apostles Bartholomew and Thaddeus, "Go into the village over there, and you will immediately find a donkey tied up, along with a colt. Release them and bring them to me. And if anyone asks you what you are doing, tell them the Lord has need of them – and they will immediately cooperate with you."

I watched as the apostles carried out the desires of their Master, and brought the animals to him. They placed their outer robes on the donkey, and then Jesus mounted the beast.

The group, with Jesus at the front, then made their way into nearby Jerusalem.

As they arrived, a large crowd assembled. As he entered through a city gate, they threw their robes on the ground in front of Jesus, and also lined his path with large palm leaves. In a spontaneous show of adoration, they said together, "Hosanna to the Son of David. He who comes in the name of the Lord is blessed – hosanna in the highest!"

Small groups broke out into singing, and many clapped their hands for joy.

In that moment of triumph, as those who worshipped and adored Jesus welcomed him into the great city with open arms and joyful respect, it seemed like everything was going to be all right.

But then I saw several Pharisees lurking in the crowd, eyeing Jesus with jealousy and disdain. They seemed repulsed by the multitude's love for Jesus.

I heard someone yell, "Who is this?"

Several in the crowd answered the man at the same time: "This is Jesus the prophet of Nazareth of Galilee."

The shouts of acclamation for Jesus warmed my heart.

For a moment, I felt like a proud father – then I remembered the reality that I was merely his custodian.

And I remembered that my pride for Jesus was

known to none but me, for I was dead and invisible.

Jesus entered the temple, and once again cast out all the merchants. Once more, he overthrew the tables of the moneychangers, and the seats of those who sold doves. "It is written that my house will be called the house of prayer, but you have made it a den of thieves!"

It was clear that he reverenced the temple as supremely holy, and that anyone found defiling it would be soundly rebuked.

Once the commotion died down, some blind and lame men came to Jesus in the temple, and he healed them. When the chief priests and scribes saw the wonderful things that he did, and the children crying out in the temple "Hosanna to the Son of David," they were greatly displeased.

"Do you hear what they say?" they asked him with scorn dripping from their lips.

"Yes," said Jesus. "Have you never read, 'Out of the mouth of babes you have perfected praise?'"

His many years of studying and memorizing the scriptures had once again been used with ultimate authority to silence his detractors.

The next day, Jesus plainly rebuked the Pharisees – openly to a large crowd.

"The scribes and the Pharisees tell you to keep the Law of Moses," he said loudly, "but they do not do so themselves. They make others work under heavy burdens, but do not lift a finger themselves. All the good they do, they do to make themselves appear righteous. They like to sit in the best seats at the synagogue, and to be called Rabbi, Rabbi. But you are all brothers and equals, and answer to one only – Christ, your Master. He who is the greatest among you shall be your servant. Whoever lifts himself up above others will be brought low, and he who is humble will be exalted. You call men on earth 'father,' but in reality there is only one who is your father – your Father in Heaven."

"Do not feel bad," said Gabriel, apparently discerning my thoughts again. "Jesus meant you no harm by his saying about fathers. He is simply trying to get men to turn to God – to see the bigger picture."

I nodded. "Yes, I understand."

Jesus continued his sermon, and delivered several sharp blows to the Pharisees, pointing out their hypocrisy.

If they were not already angry at him, by the end of this day they were seething.

But every word he said was true.

"This is important for you to see," Gabriel said as the room of the chief priests of the Sanhedrin appeared around us. "But it will be very hard for you."

The chief priests were conspiring once again, saying that their plot to kill Jesus should not be on the feast day, to avoid the people protesting.

How despicable.

Then, to my utter shock, one of Jesus' apostles, Judas Iscariot, entered the room.

"Ah," said one of the Pharisees, "Judas has come. What news do you have?"

"I can provide what you want," Judas said, his

head low. "What will you give me in exchange for delivering him to you?"

The Pharisees looked at each other, then one, the apparent leader, said, "We will covenant with you for thirty pieces of silver. That is our offer – agree, or be gone."

Judas took a moment to decide, then said quietly, "I will do it."

"What is this?" I said to Gabriel, amazed. "Judas? His apostle? Betraying Jesus?"

"I am sorry," said Gabriel, "but it is true. You are watching the downfall of a man."

"Of two men," I said bitterly.

"It shall not be Jesus' downfall," said Gabriel. "It may appear that way, but he will in fact be fulfilling his commission."

Next we found ourselves in an upper room with brown walls and a long U-shaped table.

Jesus had laid his clothing aside and put on a towel, and was washing the feet of his apostles. The greatest of all, serving these men!

When he came to Peter, the apostle tried to stop him. "Master, I worship you – you should never wash my feet."

"If you will not have me wash your feet, then you have no part with me."

Peter suddenly changed his attitude. "Then please, wash my feet, and my hands and my head as well!"

"You are already clean, except your feet. But not all are clean."

He must have been talking about Judas, for when he said that, Judas gulped and looked away – his face a picture of guilt.

He finished by saying, "If I, who you call Lord and Master, wash your feet, so then should you wash each other's feet. Service to others is one of the most important things you can do in my ministry. I have set an example for you – you will be happy if you follow it."

Jesus got dressed again. As the table was laid for supper, he said, "If you love me, you will keep my commandments. But do not fear, I will not leave you alone. My Father in Heaven and yours will send you a Comforter – which is the Holy Ghost. You will never be alone."

Then he sat to eat the Passover meal with his apostles.

Without warning, as they ate, Jesus said, "With certainty I tell you, one of you will betray me."

Everyone suddenly stopped eating and talking as a heavy feeling fell upon the room. All of the apostles looked full of sorrow.

Then each began asking, "It is me?"

"The Son of Man will fulfill all that has been written of him. But woe to that man who betrays the Son of Man! It would be better for that man if he had never been born."

"Master, is it me?" asked Judas.

"You said it," Jesus said. "What you are to do, do quickly."

Everyone turned and stared at Judas, confused. Judas looked down for a moment, ashamed. Then he turned and fled.

Simon started to go after him, but Jesus told him

not to go.

For a few moments, the apostles just stood there, breathing heavily and full of anxiety.

Changing the subject dramatically, Jesus took some bread, and broke it, and blessed it, and said as he gave it to the apostles, "Take this; eat it. This is in remembrance of my body, which I will give as a ransom for you."

Then he took a cup of new wine, and gave thanks, and gave it to the apostles, saying, "Drink all of this, for this is in remembrance of my blood of the new testament, which will be shed for as many as will believe on my name, for the remission of their sins. And I give to you a commandment that you observe to do the things which you have seen me do, and bear record of me to the very end."

All the apostles solemnly partook of the emblems.

"Now I give you a new commandment," Jesus said. "Love one another. As I have loved you, love one another. By this will men know that you are my followers, if you have love one to another."

As the words sunk in, John was moved by the spirit and began to hum a tune. Then the whole group joined in and sung the hymn together – an old song that took on new meaning for them.

> *Behold, how good and how pleasant it is*
> *For brethren to dwell together in unity!*
> *Remember all the Lord has done for you*
> *Proclaim his glory, stand up for his name*
> *Be still, and know that I am God.*
> *The Lord of hosts is with us; Selah.*

The powerful music moved my very soul.

When the singing was done, the group left the upper room and walked to the Mount of Olives.

As they neared a particular garden full of small olive tree groves, Jesus said, "All men shall be offended because of me this night. But after I have risen again, I will go before you into Galilee."

Peter, always so zealous, answered Jesus quickly. "All men may be offended because of you, but not I – I will never be offended."

"I say to you with certainty," Jesus replied, "that this night, before the cock crows, you will deny me three times."

Stunned and defiant, Peter said, "Even if it means facing death, I would not deny you."

And the other apostles agreed. "Yes, we would never deny you, Lord."

I hoped Peter would not come to regret his ardent assertion.

CHAPTER XIV – GETHSEMANE

The night seemed so dark, despite the full moon.

Clouds occasionally obscured the light it gave, but within the thick trees of the Garden of Gethsemane, it was mostly very dim.

A cool breeze caused a steady chill to strike the group as they entered into the garden.

"Sit here," Jesus told his apostles, "while I go and pray over there."

He took Peter and the sons of Zebedee, James and John, with him further into the garden. As they walked, Jesus became very heavy hearted.

"My soul is exceedingly sorrowful," he said, "I feel death hanging heavily upon me. Wait here, and watch while I go to be alone."

Jesus went on a little further. Then he fell down to his knees, and bent his face to the ground, and prayed. "Oh, my Father, if it is possible, let this cup pass from me. Nevertheless, let it not be according to my will, but yours."

After a few moments – or perhaps several

minutes – it became hard for me to tell – Jesus returned to the apostles, Peter, James and John – and they were asleep.

He said to Peter, "Could you not watch with me one hour? Watch and pray, that you do not enter temptation. The spirit is indeed willing, but the flesh is weak."

He went away again a second time, and prayed, saying, "Oh, my Father, if this cup may not pass away from me, except I drink it, then your will be done."

Once more, he returned, and found them asleep.

The poor apostles' eyes were so heavy, their strength so exhausted by the events of the evening. Jesus left them once more, knowing that he was going to have to do this completely alone.

Once more, he prayed saying the same words.

"What is he doing?" I asked Gabriel.

"This is it, Joseph. He is atoning for the sins of the world. Paying the price for every sin, every mistake, every transgression. Taking upon himself all the punishment, all the pain, all the illness and sadness and misery of the world – from the beginning of time to the end – from one end of the universe to the other. He is the ransom, the payment to appease Justice, that the Father may then offer Mercy."

"Infinite atonement," I said, my eyes transfixed on Jesus, who was once again pleading with God the Father. Perhaps hoping there was some other way – yet knowing there was not.

My mind returned to the questions of my youth – about justice and mercy, how they could possibly work together in God's plan – and suddenly it all made sense at last.

Gabriel and I stood under the trees, shaded from any light of the moon, and watched Jesus as he kneeled upon the ground, just a few paces away. I watched as he crumpled in agony. My heart broke as he prayed and shook in pain.

My tears fell to the ground in great streams from my eyes. Gabriel placed a strong hand on my shoulder as Jesus continued to writhe in incomprehensible torment.

"He suffers so," I whispered, wringing my hands and quaking uncontrollably.

I longed to comfort him, to help my son. I stepped toward him, but stopped myself, knowing I must not interfere.

I glanced around to Gabriel – but he was gone.

But I was confused for only a moment, as he immediately reappeared.

"Joseph," he said, "I have received a commandment of the Father. You are to go to Jesus." He gestured toward him. "Go."

I hesitantly moved forward; then, as Jesus fell forward on his face and quietly groaned, I hurried to him and gently placed an arm over his shoulders. I leaned close to his ear, and whispered soft words of comfort and encouragement.

He could feel me, and hear me!

He began to pray even more deeply, and he trembled as his sweat came as great drops of blood that stained his robe and fell down to the ground.

The enormity of this ultimately selfless act was impossible to comprehend. Only a god could do this. Only the Perfect One.

After what felt like an eternity, it was finally

over.

Perhaps it *was* eternity.

I returned to Gabriel, who placed his hand on my shoulder and said, "Those many years you spent wondering if you were an adequate father – now you know the truth, my friend."

As I wiped away my streaming tears, Jesus wiped the sweat and blood from his face, and wearily stood. He returned to his apostles, who saw his bloodied robes and gave him some of theirs to wear instead.

Before they could ask him questions, Jesus said, "The Son of Man will soon be betrayed into the hands of sinners. Rise, let us be going. He who will betray me is close at hand."

Before he had even finished his words, Judas came up the trail leading through the garden. Behind him followed a sizable number of men armed with swords and carrying torches that flickered in the night. They were the Sanhedrin guards, and they were moving with determination.

As Judas approached, he came to Jesus, and said, "Hail, master;" and kissed him on the cheek.

"Judas, you betray the Son of Man with a kiss?" Jesus said, clearly disappointed in the final evil deed of this man who had once been a follower worthy of apostleship.

The guards then laid hands on Jesus, and took him.

But Peter drew his sword and took a swing at the guard who was gripping Jesus' right arm. The blow severed the man's ear clean off, and blood flowed between his fingers as he slapped his hand to the side of his head, groaning in pain.

"Put away your sword," Jesus quietly said to Peter. "If you live by the sword, you will die by the sword. Besides, do you not think that I cannot pray to my Father and he would immediately send down twelve legions of angels to protect me? But then, how would the scriptures be fulfilled? No, my friend, I am to drink *all* of the cup that my Father has prepared for me."

Jesus placed his hand over the injured man's ear, and when he withdrew it, the ear was there – healed. The man stared at Jesus, tears forming in his eyes, and stepped back slowly, seeming to reconsider his decision to ally himself with the persecutors of this miraculous and kind healer.

Then Jesus turned to the armed men. "You come out here with swords to take me? I sat with you daily, teaching in the temple, and you did not lay hold on me then. What has changed?"

The men looked chastised and hesitated, but after a nod from one of the chief priests, they moved forward and took Jesus, marching him out of the garden.

I watched as the apostles all fled their separate ways.

CHAPTER XV – TRIALS

The men with swords led Jesus away to the home of Caiaphas the high priest, where the scribes and the elders of the Sanhedrin were assembled and waiting for him.

I saw Peter, following behind, out of sight. He eventually came to the priest's palace, and walked in as if he belonged there, taking a seat near some of the servants and trying to blend in.

The chief priests, and elders, and all the council, had sent out messengers to round up some false witnesses against Jesus – but got no takers. Either they could not find anyone willing to stoop so low, or they were not offering enough money.

But finally they found two people who were willing to implicate Jesus.

"Uh, yes," said the one man, looking untrustworthy and ashamed, "This man said 'I am able to destroy the temple of God, and to build it in three days.' That-that is just what he said."

The other man simply nodded then looked down quickly.

Caiaphas stood up menacingly and said to Jesus, "You have no answer to this charge? Explain what these men have said against you!"

But Jesus simply stood there and said nothing.

"I command you," said Caiaphas imperiously, "by the living God, to tell us whether you are the Christ, the Son of God."

"So you have said," Jesus replied. "But to be clear: after all this, you will see the Son of Man sitting on the right hand of power, and coming in the clouds of heaven."

In a sickening display of mock rage, Caiaphas twisted his face and ripped his clothes, moaning, "He has spoken blasphemy! What further need do we have of witnesses?" He turned to the assembled leaders, his eyes wide. "Look, now you have heard his blasphemy. What do you think?"

The wicked group murmured and several voices said aloud, "He is guilty – let him be put to death!"

Then I watched in horror as these so-called men of God – these inhuman imposters who claimed authority to lead in spiritual matters – attacked Jesus.

The filthy villains spit in his face, one after another, covering the Messiah in their disgusting venom. Then they began to riot, so it seemed, knocking Jesus around, hitting him and slapping him and mocking him. Some said such cruel things as, "Prophesy to us, Christ – who just hit you?" And they laughed together like demons.

Jesus, of course, did not fight back – did not

defend himself. He seemed to accept that this was how it was to be.

Inside, I fumed with anger at the priests, wanting to tear those wicked men away from my son and throw them across the room. My heart broke to watch my precious Jesus treated so horribly.

Finally, they seemed to tire of their game, and left Jesus alone for a few minutes while they devised details of the next step in their plan.

As the attack on Jesus dissipated, Peter, who was sitting just outside the room in the palace, was approached by a young woman.

"You were also with Jesus of Galilee," she said.

As if he'd been accused of a great crime, Peter immediately denied it. "I have no idea what you are talking about."

Looking anxious, he got up and walked away before the woman could press the issue further. He stepped outside onto the porch, and another woman saw him and said to some others who were there, "This man was also with Jesus of Nazareth."

Again, Peter, looking fearful now, said "I do not know the man."

Several minutes later, the bystanders came to Peter again, and one said, "Surely you are also one of those apostles – for your speech gives you away."

Peter got angry this time. He cursed and said loudly, "I do not know the man!" He quickly turned from the surprised questioner and began to walk away when he heard a cock crow.

He stopped in his tracks and immediately remembered the words that Jesus had spoken at the supper the night before, when he had said, "Before the cock crows, you will deny me three times."

Suddenly, a wave of misery and regret swept across Peter's face.

He left the palace in a hurry, rounded a corner to a secluded alcove set in the shadows of the wall and breathed heavily.

Then he threw his hands up to his anguished face, and wept bitterly.

Despite all his zeal, and all his vocal claims of loyalty to the Messiah, in those tense moments, he had allowed fear to trump his faith. I knew that was why he shed those tears – a feeling of personal failure. And as he wiped away the tears, I could somehow tell as I observed the resolve in his eyes that he had learned a valuable lesson – one which he would never forget.

"His heart must be broken," I whispered.

"Broken, yes," Gabriel said, "but it will mend stronger than ever."

A milky-white sun rose through a murky haze that morning, as if the darkness of night was fighting to hold back the day. Dark clouds loomed to the west, and a cold wind whipped the dust of the ground into small circling tempests.

Several of the chief priests walked out of the palace of Caiaphas, squinting as their robes flapped in the gusts. In their midst I saw Jesus, his hands bound with a thin leather strap, as if he were some kind of criminal. He was bruised about his face and neck from their barbaric assault, but his face appeared passive.

The group led him away to Pontius Pilate, the Roman governor – a thirst for blood written on their corrupt faces.

Trailing behind the group, I spotted Judas, who had betrayed Jesus.

His face was not as the chief priests. He appeared to be torn with an internal struggle.

He stopped and watched the elders as they shuffled off with Jesus. He looked as though he would weep. He turned and entered the temple, where a few of the chief priests from the group had broken off and were talking. He pulled a small bundle out of his robes.

"I – I have sinned," he told them, his hands shaking and his head hung low. "I have betrayed an innocent man."

"Why should we care?" one of the Pharisees answered gruffly. "That is your problem, not ours." They returned to their conversation, as if Judas was not even there.

Judas threw the bundle to the ground, and it broke open, spilling out the thirty pieces of silver. They made a tinkling sound as they bounced and rolled away in different directions. His face twisted in agony as he turned and ran out of the palace.

I watched him run and run, his face awash with tears, until he was beyond the city wall in a field with a few trees. Taking a rope from a nearby fence post, he threw one end up over a thick branch, tied a noose, and placed it over his head.

I looked at Gabriel. "Is he really going to take his own life? Judas – an apostle, and friend to Jesus and our family – now a betrayer. Oh, how he must feel at this moment!"

Gabriel looked ahead as Judas climbed the tree and secured the rope. Gabriel's eyes were full of wisdom and sorrow. "Judas allowed his fixation on money to overcome him when tested. He knows that. He would do better to repent and grow from this, but Satan has ensnared him. He – "

Judas cast himself down.

I winced as his body jerked to a sudden stop, and the life instantly left him.

I looked away from the tragedy. "What will become of his soul?" I asked Gabriel, who stared sadly at the still-swinging body of the former apostle.

"That is not for us to know right now," he said. "Come, let us return to Jesus."

Suddenly, we were in the governor's house – an ornately decorated mansion with tapestries adorning the walls.

Jesus stood bound before Pilate, a short Roman man with straight nose and graying hair. He asked Jesus, "Are you the king of the Jews?"

"What you say is true," Jesus answered.

The chief priests and elders started to murmur loudly, accusing Jesus of blasphemy, but Jesus did not answer them.

"Do you not hear the things these men witness against you?" Pilate asked Jesus.

But Jesus remained silent. Pilate cocked his head slightly and looked at Jesus with a combination of mild surprise, bemusement, and a hint of curious respect on his face.

He turned to one of his servants. "It is the feast

day of the Jews, is it not?"

"Yes, Governor."

"Very well. In keeping with my tradition, I will release a prisoner this day. Take this man out to the balcony, and also bring out that ghastly man they call Barabbas. I will let the Jews choose for themselves."

The servant did as he was instructed, and a few minutes later, Pilate stood upon his high balcony overlooking a large crowd in the square below. On his right hand was Jesus, on his left, Barabbas – a towering, hairy man with brute muscles and a dark emptiness in his eyes.

Pilate called out to the crowd. "Who do you want me to release to you?" He motioned to his left. "Barabbas?" And then he indicated the Messiah, on his right, "Or this Jesus, who is called Christ?"

Pilate then sat down on his throne, while the crowd chanted, cheered, and yelled – and Jesus and Barabbas stood there awaiting their fate. Pilate's wife leaned over and whispered to him, "You should have nothing to do with that just man – I had a dream today about him – it has been bothering me greatly. I know that this man is not worthy of death."

Pilate looked at her thoughtfully. "Really? Should I revoke my offer to the Jews, that they may choose for themselves?"

"I do not know," she said, "but I do know that there is something special about him – this dream was unlike any I have had and has been tormenting me."

The crowd, by this time, was becoming very

loud and unruly. Down below, the chief priests and elders were moving from person to person, whispering in their ears and stirring them up to anger against Jesus. They planted many lies in the ears of the crowd, and the men and women swallowed the falsehoods whole – even some who had witnessed the miracles of Jesus or heard his powerful teachings.

Pilate stood once again. "I ask you once more! Which of these two do you want me to release to you?"

The crowd all yelled, "Barabbas!" They began chanting his name as one.

Pilate raised his voice again, and the crowd got quieter. "And what, then, shall I do with Jesus, who is called Christ?"

"Crucify him!" one of the Pharisees called out. A few more did the same.

"Why?" asked Pilate. "What evil has he done?"

But the crowd began chanting again. "Crucify him! Crucify him!"

The bloodthirsty group got very loud and boisterous, and Pilate stopped trying to reason with them. Instead, he stepped to a bowl of water on a pedestal near his throne, and washed his hands. He stepped back to the railing and yelled down to the frenzied crowd, "I am innocent of the blood of this just person. It is on you, now."

Remarkably, the crowd screamed back, "Let his blood be upon us – and on our children!"

I could not believe my ears!

"How can they do this?" I asked Gabriel. "He has done nothing wrong! He is innocent – he is perfect! He has given of himself, healed the sick, raised the dead – he has taught them the higher law, and given them the hope of eternity. How *can* they?"

Gabriel shook his head. "It is hard to understand the evil Satan can place in the hearts of men, Joseph. But do not worry – this is all part of the great Plan."

Pilate released Barabbas to the crowd, and had his servants take Jesus away.

"What will happen now?" I asked.

"More things that will be very difficult for you to see," Gabriel said. He looked at me with a sorrowful, apologetic expression. "It will keep getting worse from here. But fear not; it is almost finished."

Before I could begin to imagine how much worse it could possibly get, I found that we were standing in a small courtyard, and I knew that it was in a section of the governor's palace.

And I did not need to imagine how much worse it could get: I was witnessing it.

Jesus, bound at the wrists, was tied to a wide wooden pole, his arms up over his head.

A Roman soldier ripped the garment from Jesus' back, exposing his skin. Another soldier, a thick-muscled man with a snarling mouth, held a vicious-looking weapon of torture: a multi-tailed whip attached to a short rod used as a handle. At the end of each of the long whips, I could see bits of sharp rocks embedded in the leather.

My stomach lurched and I cried out, *"No!"*

But nobody but Gabriel could see or hear me. The man with the whip brought it back and then flung it forward with ferocious speed.

Crack!

The whips struck my son across the back, leaving several bloody stripes.

Crack!

Once more the leather and rocks viciously sliced Jesus' skin, tearing away chunks of flesh this time. Tears sprang from my eyes and I turned away in horror, burying my head in Gabriel's chest. He put his arm around me, and I heard another blow strike Jesus, making me flinch.

Crack!

Crack!

Crack!

Oh, my God in Heaven, when will it end?

Crack!

Crack!

Crack!

Crack!

"I cannot bear any more!" I cried to Gabriel. "Take me away from this place!"

But the whipping had stopped. I turned to see Jesus unbound from the post, but his wrists still tied. The soldiers led him away into the large hall, dragging him most of the way, as he was too drained to do much more than stagger. I heard them call for other soldiers to gather round.

They shoved Jesus to the ground, where he fell to his knees, and they placed a purple robe on his back.

One soldier came in with a slender branch of thorns, which he twisted into a ring and placed on Jesus head, shoving it down hard with the flat edge of his sword. The long, sharp thorns dug into Jesus' skin, and many streams of crimson trickled down across his face, which was wet with sweat from enduring the whipping.

With the "crown" on his head, the soldiers began to mock him, saluting him and bowing down to him. Then they took a reed and started hitting Jesus on the head, and spitting on him.

My heart was ready to burst. I was filled with indignation – no, *wrath* – mixed with severe pain.

That was my baby boy; who I had once cradled in my arms, and who had grown at my side.

That was the Son of God. Perfect, loving, charitable – the Savior.

And they were beating him and mocking him!

Finally, when they had had their fill of making sport of Jesus, they removed the purple robe and put Jesus' ripped clothing back on him, and led him out of the palace.

They were heading out of the city walls – heading to the place of the skull.

CHAPTER XVI: GOLGOTHA

Jesus trudged slowly under the weight of the dark wooden cross beam, which was placed across his shoulders.

He stumbled several times, and the impatient soldiers finally grabbed a man from the side of the road and forced him to carry the cross instead.

The crowd who had called for his blood lined the pathway, taunting and jeering.

"Not so mighty now, are you?" one Pharisee called out, and chuckled.

"You will never usurp power over this people, son of a carpenter!" yelled another.

Son of a carpenter. I knew he was so much more.

So did several of the others who lined the way, supporters and followers of Jesus. They reached out and stepped forward to try to help him, but were repeatedly shoved back by the brutal Roman soldiers.

I even saw Dovev. He had apparently

abandoned any pretense of allegiance to the Sanhedrin, as tears flowed freely down his face. He even got into a brief shoving match with a Roman soldier.

The procession eventually arrived at the place called Golgotha. It was an elevated portion of land with the backdrop of a rocky foothill that had small caves that made it resemble a skull. Atop the hill, two tall poles were already jutting out of the ground, each with a thief tied to the cross bar.

The third vertical pole, which was set to be placed in the center, was still lying flat on the ground. On top of it, the soldiers fit the cross beam into a through-slot joint and secured it with a cross-tied harness, then they stripped Jesus naked and laid him on his back, his shoulders level with the cross beam.

"Nail him to it," said the leader of the Roman contingent.

A centurion pulled a bundle from a sack and tossed it on the ground next to Jesus; it landed with a clanking sound in the dust. He opened it up to reveal several very long, thick iron nails – similar to what I would use to shore up joists in my carpentry work. Without hesitation, he grabbed a large hammer, picked up a nail, and placed the pointed tip in the center of Jesus' palm.

He raised the hammer – I looked away as he brought it down with a *clink*.

Clink.

Clink.

Clink.

I looked back to see blood pouring from Jesus' hand, which was now fastened to the wooden beam.

Small specks of red – my son's blood – marked the soldier's face as he moved to the other side and repeated the torturous act on Jesus' other hand.

I saw Jesus shudder – but he let out no cries of pain.

The soldier wiped his face with the back of his hand, smearing the blood.

Next, he moved to Jesus' feet.

He placed one atop the other on the vertical beam, and pierced them with an extra-long nail.

Hammering.

Hammering.

Hammering – until only a small part of the nail could be seen protruding.

Now pinned to the wooden beams, Jesus was about to be lifted up when the Roman soldier in charge returned and said, "No, no, no – he may be thin, but the weight of his body will still cause the nails to rip right through the flesh of his hands once he has been up there for a while. We cannot have him coming down from the cross, now, can we? Or else these Jews really will think he is a god!" The men laughed at their leader's crude joke. His face turned serious. "Now, drive nails through his wrists, also, so that he is secure."

And they did so, placing the nails in such a location that they would break no bones, but support his weight and hold him sure in place.

One soldier delivered a small sign created on a piece of wood by Pilate, who stood not far off. He attached it to the cross, above Jesus' head.

THIS IS JESUS THE KING OF THE JEWS

It was written in what I could see was Greek, Latin, and Hebrew.

Some of the Pharisees complained.

"That should say, *'according to this man.'*"

"No," Pilate replied, "I have written what I have written." He gestured for the soldiers to continue with their job, and four of them lifted the cross into the upright position. Jesus' full weight now rested on the nails holding him to the cross. I saw his breathing was shallow, his sweat profuse.

They placed the bottom of the vertical pole into a hole that had been dug for it, standing the cross up, and left him there and went to gamble for his clothing, which lay on the ground.

Pilate gazed up at Jesus for a long moment, his face stern. Then he turned and walked away, not looking back.

I watched as the sky darkened, deep shadows passing across the landscape as the heavens grew more and more sinister. Strangely, there was no wind.

Those conspiring murderers of the Sanhedrin passed by, hurling insults at Jesus as he hung there.

"Ah, you who can destroy the temple and build it again in three days – save yourself, and come down from the cross!"

"He saved others, but he cannot save himself! Let Christ, the King of Israel descend from the cross now – and then we will see and believe!"

I turned to Gabriel. "Will he? Is he going to come down, and put an end to this horror?"

"No, Joseph. Do you not remember the things he has said – the things he taught? This is all part of the Plan."

"What kind of plan requires the suffering and death of a perfect man? I know what he has taught – but, I simply do not understand how this will serve a just end."

"Joseph," Gabriel said, "that is it – it is all about justice. He is answering the ends of justice – paying the price for all. He is substituting himself for all of us – for all mankind. You are witnessing justice – or, rather, the payment of justice, so that mercy can be given to all. He is completing the work he commenced in the Garden of Gethsemane last night."

I simply shook my head slowly. Yes, I did understand – but I simply *hated* that it had to be this way.

"He volunteered for this – being perfect, he is the only one who could do it," Gabriel said. "And it is his greatest happiness to please the Father and be obedient to Him in all things."

I stared at the Messiah as he hung on the cross, bleeding and trembling. "Happiness? *Happiness?* How is this happiness? It is the greatest torment, the lowest misery!"

"Have you not learned something about time during our travels together, Joseph? As devastating as this is at this moment, it will pass. And then will come rejoicing and glory."

Although it was hard to accept, I knew deep inside that he was right. Even though I now existed outside of time, part of my mind still clung to the simple ways of mortal man, with perceptions limited by time. I was not yet accustomed to living within the eternal perspective. And as his earthly father, I could not bear to watch the torturous death of Jesus – even though I could, with my mind, understand the bigger picture – my heart remained heavy as a rock.

I returned my attention to the awful scene before me, to see Jesus and the thieves on the other crosses actually talking. Then I saw someone lift a sponge of vinegar to Jesus' lips, but he would not partake of it.

The darkness had now covered the land like an oppressive blanket, and it remained that way for hours. I saw not only the mocking Pharisees and scribes present, but also some few of Jesus' followers – and his friends and family.

I saw in the crowd Mary and Martha. Martha had fallen to her knees sobbing. I also saw my other sons and daughters, all grown now, and all of whom suffered in deep sorrow. I watched as Joses – always quick to action and passion – contended with one of the Roman soldiers, as his elder brother James pulled him away.

I saw Jesus' wife Mary, their two young daughters clinging to her, their watering eyes shut tight.

I observed as Jesus spoke to his mother, and to his beloved disciple John. He told John to take care of her. Mary, along with Jesus' Mary and the girls, would be absorbed into John's household and cared for well – kept safely away from any who might try to persecute them. Surely John would do everything in his power to keep these precious women away from the wicked Pharisees or others who might try to do them harm.

More time passed, and I looked closely at Jesus'

face. His head hung forward awkwardly, and he labored to breathe. His loving eyes seemed clear, though – as if he were acutely aware of every moment of the experience.

"My son," I whispered.

Cold, hard raindrops began to drop from the roiling heavens, pelting the ground all around me, somehow missing me. But my face was bathed in salty tears that streamed uncontrollably.

Despite the aching in my soul, I could not pull myself away – as if it were my duty to force myself to watch this horrific event to the bitter end. I stared toward the hill as the sky grew an even deeper shade of gray – almost black – my stomach tight, my labored breathing ragged and shallow.

The wind picked up, and I instinctively wrapped my robe more tightly around my wiry body, though I could barely feel the sudden cold that swept from the heavens, accompanied by a fierce howling.

Most of the mocking from the riotous, bloodthirsty mob had ceased now – they had grown tired of their sport and began murmuring among themselves, many wandering off, becoming bored and wishing to escape the thickening rain and biting gusts of wind. Only the faithful, and a few Roman soldiers – remaining to fulfill their awful duty – braved the weather now.

Lightning continued to flash in the low hills around Jerusalem, briefly illuminating the olive groves and painting a milky white glow across the faces of those gathered for the crucifixion – short bursts of brightness cutting through the ever-darkening heavens.

Suddenly, at what seemed like the darkest, coldest moment, Jesus called out.

"My God, my God, why have you forsaken me?"

"Forsaken?" I asked Gabriel.

"He must do this entirely, utterly alone," Gabriel explained. "Even the Father must let him complete the mission independently."

As a father myself, I imagined that God the Father must have rushed to the other side of the universe at that moment, to hide his face from this heartbreaking scene.

I looked back at Jesus, filled with an overwhelming sense of gratitude for his strength, his obedience, and his boundless love for all mankind – for his divine goodness that enabled him to perform this sacrifice for us all.

Jesus cried out again with a loud voice. As I peered through the rain, I saw his lips move. He seemed to say, so quietly, "It is finished."

Then his head sagged forward, and he was still.

Rain drops collected and dripped from the matted strands of his hair, and from his beard.

A solemn wail emanated from the group of followers, and the clouds above boomed thunderously as nature herself groaned in savage agony.

A rush of heavy raindrops furiously showered the whole land.

My chest abruptly hollow, I gulped hard and again whispered, "My son."

"Surely this man was truly the Son of God," said a Roman soldier, as he cowered from the crashing thunder and the quaking earth.

"Indeed, he was," I said. "Indeed, he *is*."

At that moment, the world washed away around me, and I was very disoriented.

I heard Gabriel's voice in my mind. "Come, Joseph. You have a message to deliver."

Suddenly, I was standing before a man I recognized as Joseph of Arimethea – a wealthy man of the Sanhedrin that Dovev had told me was secretly a believer in Jesus. I did not know why I was standing there – but I could tell from the look of shock on the man's face, that he could see me. Then the words I was to speak came immediately to my mind.

"Joseph, I am Joseph of Nazareth. I have been sent by God. He commands you to prepare a place for the Son of Man to be laid."

"I – I have a tomb of my own," Joseph said, trembling. "I will give him my own tomb, yes. I will leave immediately to beg Pilate for the body, for the Sabbath is drawing nigh."

"Well done," I said. "Bring Nicodemus with you to help."

"Yes, it will be done," Joseph said, bowing to me.

It was fascinating to be on the giving end, rather than the receiving end, of an angelic visit.

And then the scene changed again.

CHAPTER XVII: THE MISSION CALL

I found myself seated beside Gabriel.

We were surrounded by other people – others I instinctively knew were other angels.

Before us, a clear space.

Behind us, as far as the eye could see, people were seated, ascending up like a Roman amphitheater, endlessly, fading into white light as if the heavens touched the ground.

All wore robes of the purest white; all appeared happy.

"What is this?" I asked Gabriel. "Who are these people?"

"Everyone."

"Everyone?"

"Well, all who are dead. And what this is," he gestured all around us, "it is the big one. The largest council since the Grand Council before the world was – wherein we lost one third of our brothers and sisters to the deception of the Evil One. We have all been eagerly awaiting this. It is the Great Missionary Correlation."

And we had front row seats.

I turned to the open space before us, and there he was!

Jesus.

Bright white, clean, perfect.

Glorious.

The blood and sweat and dirt had disappeared. The scratches, the bruises, the tear stains – all gone.

His robes glowed with a whiteness beyond that of the burning noonday sun. His face was passive, content.

The only evidence that he had suffered: small, clean wounds in his hands and feet.

My eyes grew wet as I took a deep breath. Unable to hold back, I rushed to Jesus and embraced him, crying on his shoulder such tears of joy. Jesus squeezed me tight and gently rubbed my back. The brief reunion over, I regained my composure, and withdrew to my seat.

Everyone around seemed to be filled with utter joy. Their quiet murmuring fell immediately silent, and he spoke.

"My friends. My brothers and sisters. My children, as you may now be called. I have completed my work on the earth; that is, my mortal ministry is finished. I have suffered all things that all men may be saved, if they come unto me."

A silent wave of enthusiasm washed over the throng.

"I now call many of you to testify of me, that the children of men may gain knowledge, and, by their faith, choose to come unto me, repent, be baptized, and endure to the end."

Through an odd sensation I had never before experienced, I felt the call – directly to my heart. I knew I had been selected to serve such a mission. I looked around, and could see that others had also felt it – they, too, had been called.

"Many of you will testify on this side of the veil, teaching the dead to believe in me and accept salvation. You will offer a chance to those who had none in mortality, or whose circumstances prevented them from having an adequate opportunity to choose. Others of you, however, will return to earth and teach and testify to the living that I am the resurrection and the life."

"Will you be there, preaching among the living?" I asked Gabriel.

"No. We will meet again, but for now, I have other work to do."

"Before you leave, I have one last question for you," I said.

"Yes?"

"Why did I have to die? I could have testified of Jesus among the living without being dead."

Gabriel smiled warmly. "You had to die, Joseph, so that Jesus – your son – could inherit the throne of David. That is all. And as you see – death is merely a doorway. All will be well. Farewell, my friend."

Those called to preach to the dead then followed Jesus and seemed to fade away from my view, including Gabriel. Jesus returned what seemed to be a moment later.

"Come," he said, looking directly into my eyes with love and joy. "It is time."

#

The spirit world seemed to fade away around me – almost completely – and I found myself standing just outside the walls of Jerusalem, near a garden tomb.

All around me, the rocks were broken up – the landscape torn and damaged. The sky was clear – the sun warm on my skin.

I had a body once again.

I was not glorified, glowing, or perfected – but I did feel very healthy – free of the chest pains that had vexed my last days, and full of life.

I looked around and saw a few others – and I understood that they were like me. One of them actually gave a small wave and smile to me. I looked closer, and saw that it was Amnun, my old beloved friend from Alexandria! A fulfillment of the word of Jesus as a little boy, when he told me I would see him again. I had not realized back then that the promise would be so long in bearing fruit.

Amnun turned and walked off. The group of missionaries – as one, yet separately – walked toward Jerusalem, each of them seeming to know where to go.

But I knew I was to stay.

I also knew there was something I was to see before I commenced my work.

I stood behind a craggy rock and looked toward the entrance to a tomb. I knew it was the tomb belonging to Joseph of Arimethea, where Jesus had been laid to rest.

The dawn grew gradually brighter, and I saw Mary, the wife of Jesus, approach the tomb, her head down, a small basket on her arm.

She had come to anoint the body of Jesus.

But the stone had been rolled away from the tomb, and the guards Pilate had placed there at the request of the Pharisees were gone.

She looked inside, and there was no body. Stifling a cry, she turned and ran. A short time later, she returned with Peter and John. Peter was out of breath, having run all the way. He looked into the tomb and confirmed what Mary had seen.

"Someone has taken him," he said, not understanding that Jesus had risen.

Peter and John then conferred and left. Mary was alone again. She kneeled by the tomb and wept. She stooped down and looked once more into the tomb, and this time she saw two angels in white. They sat at the head and the foot of the burial bed, where the body of Jesus had been.

"Why are you crying, woman?" said one angel.

"Because they have taken away my Lord, and I do not know where – where they have laid him," she said through tear-choked breaths.

She then turned around and was facing the rising sun.

And before her, in silhouette, stood the Son.

"Woman, why are you weeping? Who are you seeking?" Jesus asked, his voice soft and kind.

Against the sun, his lovely wife could not see that it was Jesus. "Sir, if you have taken him, please tell me where you have laid him, and I will take him away."

"Mary."

"Master!" she reached forward to embrace him.

"Do not touch me yet, for I have not yet

ascended to my Father. But go and tell my apostles that I have risen, and that I will ascend to our Father. Tell them they shall see me in Galilee."

Through tears of joy, Mary nodded, then hurried to tell the apostles.

His love for her was so strong, I could sense it as he watched her run off, leaving the basket of anointing spices laying on the ground. It touched me deeply that he had chosen his dear wife as the first to whom he would appear as the resurrected Savior.

He turned to me, and nodded with a small smile.

I understood.

I left, and walked to my home.

EPILOGUE

I reached the door of my house.

It felt like centuries since I had last stood there.

Perhaps it had been – for me.

I entered.

I saw Mary, and I saw John, helping her to pack some things to go and stay with his family – according to the instruction Jesus had given from the cross.

"Mary."

Her face lit up, astonished.

John's mouth dropped open.

"Joseph?" Mary asked.

"Yes, it's me," I said, smiling. "Were you expecting someone else?"

John approached me, suspicious, protective of Mary. He extended his hand.

I took it, and shook it. His face changed – he looked relieved.

"He is real," he said. "It really is Joseph." He

embraced me.

Then Mary came forward and threw her arms around me. After many long moments of her firm hug, she stepped back, her face aglow with joy and wonder. I could sense the questions swirling in her heart.

"I have been commissioned to preach the gospel," I said. "The gospel of Jesus Christ – the living Son of God."

NOT THE END

Michael D. Britton

APPENDIX

JOSEPH OF NAZARETH is a work of fiction. It's what's called "historical fiction" because the setting, characters and events are based on actual history – that is, many of the places, people and experiences related in the story *really* existed and *really* happened.

I took on the immense project of writing this book because I felt a spiritual prompting to do so. It was such a compelling and insistent prodding by the Spirit; I knew I would not be able to move forward with my writing career until I had accomplished this task. What made this work significantly different from all my other fiction writing – aside from the explicit religious nature of the content – was that it required a great deal of research in order to make it as authentic as possible.

The process of researching and writing it provided me with great personal fulfillment, as I learned so much during the time I spent preparing to write the manuscript, and then in the actual process of committing it to virtual paper.

For those who may wonder which parts of this story were research-based, what was extrapolated from research, and what was simply this writer's inspiration and creativity, I offer this appendix which references certain parts of the story, chapter by chapter, with an explanation of my research and thinking, including citations to source materials.

I do not provide this information as some sort of justification of my choices, or an attempt to "argue" a point of view. I make no apologies for what I have written, and I'm not trying to convince anyone that my novel is superior to any other account of Joseph of Nazareth. This is not the definitive story of Joseph – it's just *my* story. I hope this appendix enhances your enjoyment of the book, and answers some questions you may have as a reader. If you'd like to learn more, and draw your own conclusions, I recommend studying the publications cited, praying about it, and deciding for yourself.

Prologue

When it comes down to it, very little is known about Joseph of Nazareth, the man who raised Jesus Christ, the Savior of the World. As the most renowned step-father in all of history, he occupies a singular place as the man God selected for the life mission of teaching and protecting Jehovah during his mortal sojourn. Husband to Mary, this otherwise-ordinary carpenter from an obscure village in Palestine must have been one of the noble and great ones in the pre-existence, foreordained to this magnificent calling.

Although he knew from the start that Jesus was not his own, literal son; he loved him with all the tender feelings of any father, and surely must have felt the weight of his breathtaking responsibility to take good care of Jesus.

Having learned from Jesus for years, he would have had some understanding of the Plan of Salvation, and Jesus' central role in it. Still, as a man of his own time, he would have likely not fully understood every aspect of the Atoning Sacrifice of the Lamb of God – even Christ's own apostles, called and set apart to the work, did not quite "get it" at first. Surely, watching Jesus suffer on the cross would have been profoundly heartbreaking for this good father, Joseph. Even knowing the Plan, to watch your own (grown) child suffer in that manner had to be an excruciating experience.

An explanation of why Joseph was not with Mary and *among* the mourners can be found in the notes for Chapter XVI.

Chapter I – Falling for Mary

Most young Jewish men of that era married around the age of seventeen.[4] Refer also notes for Chapter XI.

It was typical to learn one's father's trade in preparation for adulthood and being the head of a family.[4]

We know from various scriptures that the stoning of young women suspected of inappropriate sexual behavior occurred in these times.[1] However, we also know that the Jews of the time had established many strict rules, ordinances and punishments that were at variance with the spirit of the law.[1,2] It is reasonable to believe that not all men of the time were in agreement with the way the laws had been changed over the generations; even faithful Jewish men may have recognized the injustice and barbarity of some of the cultural norms extant. However, conformity (or, at least, the general appearance thereof) was expected.

Young women of that era were typically married in their early teens.[4] It was common for marriages to be arranged between relatives (such as distant cousins). The custom was for the groom's family to pay a dowry to the family of the bride, since the family of the bride would be losing a useful member of the household. The value of the dowry would be negotiated by the heads of household.[4]

The betrothal was considered a more significant event than the actual wedding. The celebration was more elaborate, and the act of betrothal was believed to be a truly binding contract – more than a mere "engagement" of today. Betrothed couples were, for all intents and purposes, "married," though consummation of that marriage was, of course, forbidden until after the official wedding.[4]

Chapter II – Silent Scandal & Vocal Revelation

Here, where Gabriel speaks to Joseph, we have the first instance of dialog taken from the New Testament.[1] I chose to make minor alterations to the text, rather than use direct quotations, because I did not want to throw the reader out of the story by jumping into and out of King James style language. You could say I made my own translation from the King James. I did this because I do not particularly like the more modern translations available today; and even if I did, they would not likely be a perfect match for the style of language in which I wrote this book (a mostly formal, somewhat archaic style that blends older linguistic modes with more modern phraseology).

At first, I was going to produce my own translation of the New Testament from original sources. I even purchased books on how to learn Hebrew. But further study led me to believe that would be a foolish (and impossible) endeavor. For starters, the original language spoken then and there was Aramaic. To properly translate, I would need to be fluent in Aramaic, Hebrew and Greek. Second, there are no "original sources" in existence.[3] The best sources that scholars have consist of a few tiny papyrus fragments that date to many decades (in some cases, centuries) after the time of Jesus. Since I am not interested in changing careers, I decided it would be acceptable to simply use slight modifications of the King James version, which, in conjunction with the Joseph Smith translation, is our most reliable source. I strove to not take too many liberties in this respect. However, despite my extensive research, I'm not a scholar of antiquity; I am a fiction writer first and foremost.

It should also be noted that there is no definitive record of the identity of the angel who spoke to Joseph on this and other occasions.[1] The assumption that it was Gabriel was an authorial choice designed to make the story more cohesive from a character standpoint.

Later in this chapter, Mary recounts her experience with Gabriel. This is a case of a character paraphrasing an event that we have recorded in scripture.[1] This occurs frequently in the first portion of this novel, as the story is told strictly from Joseph's point of view; so in order to be apprised of certain events, he must receive the accounts second-hand (until Chapter XIII, when Joseph's perspective gets a supernatural boost).

Chapter III – Marriage and a Journey

The wedding did not receive much "screen time" in this story – partly as a reflection of how hastily it came about, and partly because, as previously noted, the wedding was generally less significant an event than the betrothal in that culture.[4]

Mary's visit to Elizabeth occurs at this point in the story because sequence can be difficult to determine based solely on the scriptural accounts.[1] For example, while the Gospel of Luke gives an account of the visit, the other Synoptic Gospels (Matthew and Mark) and John are silent on the subject. Likewise, there are events recorded by John that do not appear in the Synoptic Gospels. In cases like these, it can be difficult to determine the exact sequence of events, while still possible to infer the general time line.[3]

Although it is not recorded that Joseph accompanied Mary, she would not have traveled alone, and since I wanted to include the events of the visit, it was advantageous to place Joseph in the scene, so he would not have to get the information second hand (remember, all of the events in the book are from his point of view).

Chapter IV – The Birth of Jesus

The weather described in this chapter is reflective of early April in the Bethlehem vicinity (according to dating of Jesus' birth to April 6).[8]

Salt was used to cleanse newborn infants at birth.[4]

The concept that Joseph was the first to hold the Messiah (since he delivered the Babe) inspired a poem I wrote in December of 2009. That poem (along with spiritual promptings) inspired the idea to write this book. It is copied below:

Joseph Delivered the Deliverer

Joseph was told in a sacred dream
Of the Life entrusted to his care
He stood beside Mary and took care of her
An outstanding man, and his wife so fair

Joseph delivered the Deliverer
Into his calloused young hands came He
Joseph helped raise that little Boy
Who was raised after three days for you and for me

Joseph witnessed the sacred event
The Babe as He entered this mortal realm
Present at the start of the new dispensation
Receiving the ultimate Present to o'erwhelm

Joseph delivered the Deliverer
And protected his new family
Joseph, the greatest step-father of all
Held such a sacred responsibility

Chapter V – Unexpected Visitors

This visit from the shepherds is based on the account found in the second chapter of Luke.[1] There is very little deviation from the source material.

Chapter VI –Infancy

Details such as the typical layout of an "inn" – or caravansary – came from an address by Elder Russell M. Nelson of the Quorum of the Twelve Apostles.[7]

Here, we have another reference to the weather, consistent with early April in Bethlehem.[8]

Chapter VII – A Hasty Escape

I chose to set the time of the visit of the Wise Men at approximately two years after the birth of Jesus Christ. This accords well with the scriptural account of their warning the family about Herod, and the subsequent Slaughter of the Innocents.[1] I selected five Wise Men, rather than the traditional three, simply because there is no record of the specific number of visitors.[9,10] I used the term "olibanum" rather than "frankincense" because it is more appropriate for that time and place. (Wikipedia)

Chapter VIII – Life Among the Pyramids

The exile of the family to Egypt is a subject that has received almost no coverage. But a good deal of time was spent there, after what must have been a difficult journey, so I decided to include this part of the life of Joseph in my narrative. It surely would have produced anxiety in Joseph and Mary to know that a powerful ruler with many men at his disposal was out to get them, to try to kill the precious infant Jesus.[1]

Upon arrival in Egypt, they needed a place to stay, and I chose Alexandria as it was the city that, at that time, was most likely to be a safe harbor for Jews. The Shamar district was my own fabrication. Likewise, Amnun and his family – and all other experiences Joseph had in Egypt – were of my own creation, with the exception of his being told in a dream[1] that it was time to return to Nazareth. I placed their time in Egypt at a duration of two years, since that information is also unavailable in the source materials and can only be speculated by scholars. It also correlates well with the probable lifespan (death date) of Herod.

Chapter IX – A Heartbreaking Return

As Joseph and his family left Egypt, I included a little prophecy from the young Jesus, to show that even in his youth he was divine and prophetic, and capable of providing comfort.

This brief chapter dealt mainly with the fact that upon their return to Judea, they would have found that a fresh, open wound remained in that land that had been robbed of all of its infant boys just two years earlier, when Herod had had so many murdered.[1] That generation of Jews would forever have a huge gap in Jesus' age cohort, and in their hearts.

Chapter X – A Scare, and a Reminder

Zacharias was indeed killed during the slaughter of the baby boys; we also know that John had escaped the murderous rampage and grew up in the wilderness.[1] During Jesus' childhood, Joseph and Mary continued to have additional children – half-brothers and half-sisters to Jesus – as was typical for any Jewish family of the day. There are some Christian religions that claim Mary remained a virgin until death, but such a claim runs counter to the New Testament account of Jesus' siblings, some of whom are even named in the scriptures.[1] In addition to the names provided scripturally, I added some more of my own creation. The number of children is appropriate to the likely duration of time between pregnancies for a Jewish family of that era, due to customs regarding nursing.[4]

Joseph's experience with Jesus as a child (and even his friend Amnun's recognition in Egypt that Jesus was a very special and unusual child) correlates with what Elder Bruce R. McConkie has said about Jesus' youth: *"And as with our Lord's physical growth and development, so with his mental and spiritual progression. He learned to speak, to read, to write; he memorized passages of scripture, and he pondered their deep and hidden meanings. He was taught in the home by Mary, then by Joseph, as was the custom of the day. Jewish traditions and the provisions of the Torah were discussed daily in his presence. He learned the Shema, reverenced the Mezuzah, and participated in prayers, morning, noon, and night. Beginning at five or six he went to school, and certainly continued to do so until he became a son of the law at twelve years of age. On Sabbaths and on weekdays he attended the synagogue, heard the prayers and sermons, and felt the spirit of the occasion. He participated in the regular worship during the feasts, particularly at*

Passover time. Indeed, the whole Jewish way of life was itself a teaching system, one that made the Jews a unique and peculiar people, a people set apart from all the nations of the Gentiles. It is also apparent that Jesus learned much from nature – from observing the lilies of the field, the birds of the air, and the foxes that have holes for homes. It seems perfectly clear that our Lord grew mentally and spiritually on the same basis that he developed physically. In each case he obeyed the laws of experience and of learning, and the rewards flowed to Him. The real issue of concern is not that he grew and developed and matured – all in harmony with the established order of things, as is the case with all men – but that he was so highly endowed with talents and abilities, so spiritually sensitive, so in tune with the Infinite, that his learning and wisdom soon excelled that of all his fellows. His knowledge came to him quickly and easily because he was building as is the case with all men upon the foundations laid in preexistence. He brought with him from that eternal world the talents and capacities, the inclinations to conform and obey, and the ability to recognize truth that he had there acquired. Mozart had musical ability at the age of six that only a handful of men have ever gained in a whole lifetime. Jesus, when yet a child had spiritual talents that no other man in a hundred lifetimes could obtain."

The account of Jesus being left behind in Jerusalem is given further realism by the fact that the family's caravan would have been fairly large, with siblings and extended family in attendance – thus making it easier for Jesus' absence to go unnoticed for a few hours. We have read the brief account in the New Testament many times, but I was glad to have the opportunity to recount it from the point of view of the frantic, worried parents. Losing a child is a parent's worst fear; losing the Messiah must have been even more terrifying for Joseph and Mary.

Chapter XI – Doubts & Miracles

In this chapter, Joseph and Mary discussed their questions and concerns about Jesus' future; how his life would play out as the Messiah. Mary pointed out that Jesus knew and kept the law perfectly – and for young Jewish men, that would include marrying and having a family.[4] The idea that Jesus would not marry is simply incompatible with his life as an obedient and exemplary Jewish man. It is also incongruent that our Perfect Exemplar would *not* be our exemplar in the two most important roles for any man: being a husband and father. He whose priesthood it is would certainly have fulfilled the most important roles of a priesthood holder.

In support of this conclusion, I note here that several leaders of The Church of Jesus Christ of Latter-day Saints have affirmatively taught that Jesus was in fact married during mortality. For example, Elder Orson Hyde believed that the marriage in Cana, found in the New Testament, was in fact Jesus' marriage: "It will be borne in mind that once on a time, there was a marriage in Cana of Galilee; and on a careful reading of that transaction, it will be discovered that no less a person than Jesus Christ was married on that occasion."[11]

While Elder Bruce R. McConkie did not draw such an explicit conclusion, he did note that, "Mary seemed to be the hostess at the marriage party, the one in charge, the one responsible for the entertainment of the guests. It was she who recognized the need for more wine, who sought to replenish the supply, who directed the servants to follow whatever instructions Jesus gave. Considering the customs of the day, it is a virtual certainty that one of Mary's children was being married...Jesus also had a close personal interest in and connection with the marriage and the subsequent festivities which attended it. He and apparently at least five of his disciples (John, Andrew, Peter, Philip, and Nathaneal) were "called" to attend. Since the shortage of wine occurred near the close of the festivities, and since these commonly lasted from seven to fourteen days, it is apparent that Jesus' party was remaining for the entire celebration. Seemingly, also, he had some personal responsibility for entertaining the guests and felt an obligation to supply them with added refreshments."[12]

The implicit evidence regarding the marital status of Jesus is far greater than the explicit evidence. Scholar Sidney B. Sperry noted, "[W]e know that it was the custom among the Jews for their young men to marry at an early age, generally between the years of sixteen and eighteen. And secondly, it is well known that the Jews considered marriage to be a religious obligation."[13]

Elder Bruce R. McConkie also noted, "Men married at sixteen or seventeen years of age, almost never later than twenty: and women at a somewhat younger age, often when not older than fourteen.[14] Marriage is vitally important in Judaism.

Refraining from marriage is not considered holy, as it is in some other religions. On the contrary, it is considered unnatural. The Talmud (referred to in this chapter as the Mishnah, which forms part of the basis of the Talmud) says that an unmarried man is constantly thinking of sin (as Mary is heard to mention in this chapter). The Talmud recommends that a man marry at age 18, or somewhere between 16 and 24.[15]

While there is no definitive evidence that Jesus was a husband and a father, it flies in the face of reason and intuition to deny that he was. I did not include this information in this story to be controversial – I included it because it was a natural part of expanding the historical picture beyond what's found in the scriptures, which are, by their nature, very limited.[3]

I selected Mary of Magdala (commonly known now as Mary Magdalene) to be the wife of the Savior. I made this choice based on a number of historical/biblical clues that make her a very likely candidate. Unlike some contemporary interpretations, Mary was not a prostitute or a woman of any ill repute; in fact, as a devout disciple of Jesus she was surely a woman of great virtue. According to the New Testament record, Mary was frequently found to be near Jesus at various points during his ministry, she was present at his crucifixion, and she was the first person to whom he appeared as the resurrected Lord – surely his wife would be the logical choice for these pivotal roles. Mary is mentioned by name at least 12 times in the four Gospels – more than most of the apostles. While there is much in the way of inconclusive scholarly speculation on Mary, most of it dates to many hundreds of years after her lifetime, thus making my choice here no less valid.

Also in this chapter, I decided to move Joseph and his family from Nazareth to Jerusalem, as that is where the majority of the remainder of Jesus' life plays out, and I needed to keep Joseph close so he could be a witness to those important events.

For Jesus' wedding at Cana, I thought it would be interesting to have Joseph be the one who forgot to bring the extra wine, leading to the first recorded miracle in the New Testament – the changing of the water to wine.

Finally, I chose to make both of Jesus' children girls, so there would be no male heir issue to complicate whatever readers may choose to speculate regarding his progeny.

Chapter XII – His Ministry Begins

Here we have the baptism of Jesus (and of Jesus' entire extended family, as one might expect to have happened). We also have the first of two times that Jesus cleansed the temple of merchants.[1] Jesus account of his temptations in the wilderness during his forty day fast is retold by him, in the first person, but uses the Joseph Smith translation to clarify that it was not Satan who was moving him from place to place, but the Spirit.[2]

This portion of the story follows Jesus through many of his recorded sermons and miracles. I placed the character of Dovev in many of these scenes in order to provide a unique viewpoint: a man of the Sanhedrin (who would naturally be skeptical of the Messiah); a good man whose faith can overcome his doubts; a man who has split loyalties, between his friendship with Joseph and the family of the Messiah, and the powerful socio-religious group he had worked hard to join. The character of Dovev allows the reader to witness an unfolding conversion over a period of time – including some description of his understanding of Jesus' profound words. Dovev also served the vital narrative purpose of feeding information from the Sanhedrin to the first-person protagonist, Joseph, who would not have otherwise known what the Pharisees were up to. This is why I selected the name "Dovev," which, in Hebrew, means "whisper."[17]

At the end of this chapter, Joseph dies. It's not common to kill off your protagonist three quarters of the way through a book, but since death is not the end, neither does the story end here. It was necessary to have Joseph die at this juncture, because (as Gabriel explains near the end of the book), Jesus could not inherit the throne of David if Joseph (the rightful heir) remained alive.[16] Also, it helps to account for Joseph's absence from the New Testament accounts of the crucifixion. Further, Joseph's crossing to the other side of the veil allowed for him to have a more "omniscient" or "third person" viewpoint (fiction terminology). This greatly enhanced the opportunities to tell parts of the story to which Joseph would have otherwise not been privy.

Chapter XIII – The Other Side of the Veil
Here the story continues to follow Jesus through much of his ministry, but without the

constraints of Joseph's mortality. This section mirrors the previous one in the sense that Joseph often brought Dovev along to learn of Jesus; while now, Gabriel is bringing Joseph along to train him for his upcoming mission.

When Gabriel allowed Joseph to look in on his family, I chose to portray Mary as ever-faithful, even with the passing of Joseph. She had experienced so much over the last thirty to thirty-five years – I wanted to show her as being strong and having a balanced spiritual perspective.

In this chapter, we also witness the transfiguration. Although there is no specific description of the conception of Jesus in the scriptures or in this book (beyond the terminology "overshadowing by the Holy Ghost"), because the term "overshadowed" is used to describe the transfiguration, I believe that what occurred at the conception was also a transfiguration – the transcending of the veil similar to the way Gabriel describes the event on the mount with the apostles. However, since Joseph wasn't present for that, it is not in this book.

In the case of the rich young man who Jesus told to give away all his possessions, I gave the man a name, and also had Dovev continue to teach the man after he went away sorrowing. Dovev's lesson about the "Eye of the Needle" is an intentional conflation of several apocryphal tales about such a place. There is no evidence of this scripturally – it was of my own creation.

I also showed a glimpse of Judas – what he experienced in his conflicted nature as the betrayer. He held a special position as an apostle, so surely his choice to sell Jesus out came as the result of his falling to his biggest temptation: money. More than once, he showed his weakness for financial considerations. And as we see later, he regretted that failure so much that he took his own life. Truly a tragedy, and a lesson for all.

The hymn sung after the Last Supper[1] is one that I made up. The first couplet is from Psalm 133, the middle couplet is of my own creation, and the last couplet is from Psalm 46.[1] The line about standing up for the Lord's name is intended to foreshadow Peter's triple denial. We can only imagine what the music was like – it must have been very moving.

Chapter XIV – Gethsemane

What happened in the garden was the pivotal and defining moment of all human history. The scriptures record that as Jesus suffered, he was comforted by an angel.[1] In what I can only call a moment of pure inspiration – a feeling that I will always hold sacred – I realized that the perfect angel for that role was none other than Joseph himself, the earthly father of Jesus. This tender moment of father comforting son during the deepest of trials remains my favorite part of the entire book. I hope it moved you as it did me.

Chapter XV – Trials

This chapter contains is very little deviation from the source material – I mostly took what's found in the New Testament and fleshed it out.[1]

Chapter XVI – Golgotha

It is unclear from the scriptural record why Jesus chose John to care for his mother, Mary.[1] It is likely that Jesus' sisters were already married and living in their own households, and his brothers may have been tapped to go on missions following the resurrection.

Jesus' brother James is also present; he later became a Christian leader in Jerusalem (see Galatians 1:19).

I chose to have Joseph deliver the charge to Joseph of Arimethea to donate his tomb.[1] It is not specified that the benefactor was called to do so, but I wanted to give Joseph the opportunity to be an angelic message deliverer.

Chapter XVII – The Mission Call

The events of this chapter form my own portrayal of that which took place according to latter-day revelation.[18] We also know from the New Testament that Jesus organized the preaching of the gospel during his three days of death.[1] It only makes sense that Joseph would be present for that, and also that he would be selected as one of the many people who were resurrected at the time of Jesus' resurrection. It further made sense to me that those who were resurrected did so because they had a calling to preach the gospel. After all, what else would a person do after coming back from the dead?

Epilogue

In this final scene, John ensures that Joseph is indeed real by shaking his hand. This is an allusion to the instructions found in latter-day revelation.[19] Joseph's words to Mary echo the in-joke they had shared between them dating back to the day they met, bringing the story full-circle.

Finally, there are the names in the book. Nearly 100 individual characters appear in JOSEPH OF NAZARETH. Approximately half of them are named in the scriptures. A few others are mentioned, but not by name. The rest are figments of my (and now your) imagination. Many of my fictional characters received their names for specific reasons; here are a few of them:

While the scriptures do provide us with the names of some of Jesus' half-siblings (James, Joses, Simon, & Judas), we do not know the others. I gave them the names Abish, Hannah, Ruth and Benjamin because the latter three are nice, standard biblical names, while "Abish" is an homage to the Abish found in the Book of Alma.

I named Joseph's mother Sariah in honor of the wife of Lehi (mother of Nephi), another great mother. One of Joseph's sisters is named Deborah, a biblical name, and also the name of my wife's mother (another great mother). Mary's father is named Amram, which is a Hebrew name which means "kindred of the Most High." Seemed appropriate.

Joseph's close friend and confidant over the years, the Pharisee fence-sitter named Dovev, is the man who whispers to Joseph about the doings of the Sanhedrin. Dovev is a Hebrew name which means "whisper."

The officiator at Jesus' wedding was Rabbi Chaim; this Hebrew name means "life."

The father of Mary Magdalene is Chinan, which is a Hebrew name meaning "gracious." Her mother Shula's name means "peaceful." The names of the daughters of Jesus and Mary, Malka and Eliora, mean "queen" and "my God is light," respectively.

The names of the wise men are not given in the scriptures, though I did use the traditional names for three of them: Melchyor, Caspar, and Balthazar. The other two are named Rentha and Denji in this book; both of these are names I made up. They seemed like good ancient, foreign names for great men from distant lands.

In Egypt, Joseph's friend is named Amnun, which is actually the name of a Hebrew settlement in Upper Galilee that was formed to accommodate Jewish evacuees following the Egypt-Israel Peace Treaty of 1979. His wife's name is Amina, which is a Hebrew name meaning "faithful, trusted." Their twin boy and girl are Elazar and Anat, Hebrew names meaning "God has helped" and "answer to prayer," respectively. Since this family was of great assistance to Joseph and his family while they were in Egypt as "evacuees," those names all seemed fitting.

Elad, Joseph's business partner, is the name of a man in Israel for whom I did some freelance writing work. I just liked the name.

Nachum - a rich young follower of Christ, is referred to in the scriptures, but not by name. I gave him this name because it is a Hebrew name which means "comfort." This young man took comfort in his material belongings, but after being disappointed with the Master's admonition to leave them behind, Dovev provided him a comforting lesson.

Lastly, I also made up a place name: the Shamar. This was the district in Alexandria set apart for Jewish expatriates. Shamar is a Hebrew word which means "to be kept, to be guarded." This is appropriate for a place of refuge where Joseph and his family were kept safe during Herod's reign of terror.

SOURCES:

1. The gospels according to Matthew, Mark, Luke & John; The New Testament, King James Version (The Church of Jesus Christ of Latter-day Saints, 1981)

2. The gospels according to Matthew, Mark, Luke & John; The New Testament, Joseph Smith Translation (The Church of Jesus Christ of Latter-day Saints, 1981)

3. Jesus Christ and the World of the New Testament: An Illustrated Reference for Latter-day Saints, by Richard Neitzel Holzapfel, Eric D. Huntsman, and Thomas A. Wayment (Shadow Mountain, 2006)

4. Ancient Hebrew Social Life and Custom as Indicated in Law, Narrative and Metaphor, by R. H. Kennett (Oxford University Press, London, 1933)

5. The Four Gospels, by D. Kelly Ogden and Andrew C. Skinner (Deseret Book, 2006)

6. Mary, the Mother of Jesus, by Camille Fronk Olson (Deseret Book, 2012)

7. "The Peace and Joy of Knowing the Savior Lives," Elder Russell M. Nelson, *Ensign*, December 2011

8. President Harold B. Lee, in *Conference Report*, April 1973.

9. "We Three Kings," by Wendy Kenney, *New Era Magazine*, December 2009

10. "What Do We Know about the Wise Men?" by John A. Tvedtnes, from *Insights: An Ancient Window* (newsletter of the Foundation for Ancient Research and Mormon Studies [FARMS]), December 1998.

11. Journal of Discourses, Vol.4, p.259 – expand entry

12. Doctrinal New Testament Commentary, Vol.1, p.135 – expand

13. Paul's Life and Letters, p.9 – expand

14. The Mortal Messiah, Vol.1, p.223 – expand

15. http://www.jewishvirtuallibrary.org/jsour
ce/Judaism/marriage.html

16. From a personal interview with an expert;
an experienced seminary instructor and
mission president.

17. http://www.20000-
names.com/male_hebrew_names_02.htm

18. See Doctrine & Covenants 138:27-37

19. See Doctrine & Covenants 129

*Additional background information was obtained
from the Neal A. Maxwell Institute, various General
Conference and BYU talks by general authorities, the
official LDS website LDS.org, the unofficial LDS website
LightPlanet.com, Wikipedia, and Google Maps.*

ABOUT THE AUTHOR

Michael D. Britton has been writing professionally for nearly 25 years, working in government, private industry, marketing, technical, web, freelance and a decade in the raw world of TV news.

His short fiction has received multiple honorable mentions in the Writers of the Future contest, among other recognition; and his novels have advanced through multiple rounds of the Amazon Breakthrough Novel Award in various years. His list of titles exceeds 70 and keeps increasing.

Find more books by Michael D. Britton at

www.michaeldbritton.com

Michael D. Britton

Made in the USA
Charleston, SC
09 October 2014